Junie's Red Carpet

C.C. Troy

TouchPoint
Press

JUNIE'S RED CARPET
Published by TouchPoint Press
2075 Attala Road 1990
Kosciusko, MS 39090
www.touchpointpress.com

Editor: Tamara Trudeau
Cover Design: Colbie Myles, colbiemyles.com

Dedication

For those who create love and fun in all circumstances.
Thank you.

Section One: The Twist of Fate

"Junes!" Greg called as he hurriedly piled several large pizza boxes on top of each other. The pies they contained were so hot; the teenager had to fan his fingers in the air as he added to the stack. "He's got a stop watch on you! I was thirty seconds late last time, and we had to give him a free one! Tony and Alberto still yell at me for it. Come on! Eat that later!"

Junie bit off a large piece of cheese pizza and took a gulp of soda. She came over to Greg at the counter with a bloated mouth and twinkling eyes as she accepted the delivery ticket and pungent delights. Scanning the address on the stub, she pushed it into the money apron around her waist. She looked at him with amusement as she could tell the lanky high school senior had more to say.

"Remember, he's a really *old* dude, retired a zillion years ago from…whatever. He was a big wig of some kind, and he and the other guys live in this monster house that was built by the pilgrims, or something, but it's *old*. Every*thing* and every*one* in there is old, old, *old,* so just be ready for that. I mean, they make my Grandpa look like he should be in kindergarten, that's how old they are. It grossed me out the first time I saw them, but don't let on because you can get a good tip if you act like it doesn't bother you.

"When you get there, you have to push a button on the intercom on the outside of the gate. Big Wig Dude will talk to you like he's still in a tank, and you're both in the water, and he's going to sink you if he doesn't like you, or something. What are you laughing at, Junes? Don't snort like that when you have food in your mouth! I can't look at you now! Just go along with whatever he says because he won't let you in if you don't play the game, and you'll come back here and have to pay for their food out of your own pocket because WE KNOW HOW GENEROUS TONY AND ALBERTO ARE!" Greg scowled with an intensity to go along with his harsh tone, but he knew his bosses couldn't hear him. The hostess did frown at them as she was about to seat a family in one of the larger booths around the corner from where they were stationed.

It wasn't a good day for Greg. Junie, his elder by seven years, understood why. The day before he had badly twisted his ankle playing soccer, and he not only was benched for weeks from his favorite sport, but Tony and Alberto told him if he called out again, he only need return to collect his last paycheck. Temporarily in a hard cast because his injury was so profound, Greg was uncomfortably perched on a stool earning his minimum wage salary any way they deemed. Now he would be without tips as well, which only added to the sting of his circumstances.

Junie was Tony and Alberto's star waitress. Employed by the brothers since Greg's age, she covered her five p.m. to one a.m. shift without deviation. It was her second job of the day, yet her energy level was usually high and jovial, and her knowledge of the menu and what the brothers would accommodate for special requests was unparalleled. In her career there, she had filled every position except deliveries, but that changed on this night. With Greg out of commission and no replacement available, she had been elected to cover the entire area the restaurant provided to. Junie felt worse for him than for herself, though she had twice the work to do.

Her younger friend whined: "I told you all this, so you've got to split your tip with me, Junes! That's only fair. I don't know how many times it took me to learn how they want things. Come on, I usually make five bucks at least there!" He watched her as she swallowed more soda, and slapped on the required dull green cap for the establishment's advertising. She wriggled the brim down to her eyebrows, and gathered the boxes to go out the side door. She winked at him as she went out backside first.

"Junie! I didn't have any warning like this, come on!" she heard as the door closed behind her. With her large mouthful of soda safely dispatched, she was able to laugh as she teased him by wrinkling her nose and shaking her head as a negative response. Through the glass of the door, she was able to see him make a fist and pound it on his knee, hurting the very leg that had sidelined him. It appeared he wasn't happy about this, either, and it made her laugh once more.

With the aromatic provisions in the front seat, Junie put her small car into gear and said a quick prayer it would keep struggling for a few more hours. The upholstery was mainly grey duct tape, it had better not rain, the radio received one station when it wanted to, and she was sure if the front end was ever properly aligned, the vehicle would stop working altogether. At least the weather was appealing to her.

Taking the order slip out of the apron, she glanced at it again. The address she and the pizzas were going to was 60 Pond Point Avenue. She had been by the street before, but never had cause to traverse it. She knew it to be in the historic section of her town, and while there were many founder's homes there, she chuckled as she knew the pilgrims were not the craftsmen.

After a short few minutes of her car rattling along at a good pace, Junie turned down the wide, smoothly paved road without a problem. The grass was certainly greener due to the landscaping agency's care, and brick and iron fences with flowering trees and bushes were the norm. Her car backfired as if unimpressed, but she didn't concur. She even cranked down the window to inhale the sweeter air. Slowing her pace, she jolted, suddenly recalling she wasn't there for a pleasant outing, and she patted the boxes next to her and began looking for the specific address. While the standard rule dictating odd house numbers on one side and evens on the other held true, nothing seemed consecutive, and houses next to each other jumped by as much as fifty digits as she advanced. A cast iron oval with the number sixty painted in a glossy white beckoned her.

She turned onto the beige-pebbled drive and was stopped by a black gate. It seemed unusually high, but "Oh, my…" she breathed as her focus went past the dented hood immediately in front of her to the house. Beyond the simulated spears of the road access laid a circular drive with a fountain dressed with spring bulbs. An expansive white house in a federal style loomed thereafter—an entire three stories of it—with coal-black shutters and a matching gable roof. The flower beds and trees were perfectly groomed, appearing to know they were fortunate to surround the structure. The smaller panes of the windows told on its age, but it was a highlight, not a hindrance, as someone of Greg's limited years couldn't understand. As the scene before her wasn't pretentious, her gentle character was further

4

warmed.

"So many purchases, so little inheritance," Junie joked with a smile, then remembered the infamous stop watch. She turned to her left and found the call box. Taking a deep breath in anticipation, she realized she would be disappointed if whom she had been told of didn't answer. She pressed the call key and waited, smiling.

"Friend or foe, I ask of you out there! Hoist your colors and identify yourself, or all cannons at hand will be positioned for a warning shot across your bow!" came the spirited voice through the speaker.

Junie laughed, happily fulfilled. She could see why Greg had been taken aback during his first visit, and she promised to give him the entire tip. To have some unique fun and perhaps see some of the house would be bonus enough for her. This alone was worth the strain of the night. Drawing from odd phrases she heard on television through the years, she readied her reply.

"Ahoy, sir! I claim myself to be a friend, arriving with rations for the crew. I have five deliveries sent at full cruising speed from 'Uncle Tony's Pizza and Subs'. Permission requested to come aboard!" She was certain she hadn't made any sense at all, but she so enjoyed daring herself to follow through, she was prepared for a full scolding.

Instead came: "Permission granted! Well done out there, whoever you are! Upon entry, I will give you a sound toot. Perhaps two! Yes, I think so. Two it is!"

Junie laughed as the box went silent. The electric power of the gate buzzed loudly, and the bars began to move. They creaked as they should, and she smiled for having the privilege of approved passage. Her car's tires crunched musically over the pebbles, and she passed a row of six garages to her left. She was sorry she reached a proper parking spot as soon as she did, and she came to a slow stop just past the wide brick patio that was part of the decorative front entry. She wanted to go around the circle at least once, and she would have if she were not being observed.

She put her car in park, leaving the ignition engaged in case it didn't want to turn over again in a few minutes. She went to the passenger door to retrieve the heavy items that were the reason for her journey.

The front door opened, and a very slim elderly man, nimbly in command of his wheelchair, came forward. He wore thick, round glasses beneath his balding pate that were so magnifying, the lenses seemed nothing but a blinking blue. He wore a crisp pair of white tennis shorts, spotless crew socks, sneakers, and a bright red tee-shirt with the screen print of "Seventy Rules!" boldly across the chest.

"Greetings, fine, young, new pizza deliverer!" was spoken with great aplomb. "I promised you two toots for your wit, and you shall have them! Advance!"

A smiling Junie went over to the entry and stood before him. On the one arm of his wheelchair was secured a rubber ball attached to a bicycle horn. The horn was screwed into the left arm of the chair, and it had to be as he utilized it with a great wrenching. Even expectant of it, the noise was blaring. She might have been able to hear it off the property.

"Thank you, sir!" she replied as she nodded her brim in respect. Carefully balancing the boxes on one palm, she used her free hand to bring her auburn hair behind her back.

He bowed to her with his shining head. "The conversation was ship-shape, for a land-lubber, that is! I sincerely hope I'll have the pleasure of schooling you in the fine art of Navy terminology. Did Gregory, our normal fine, young, delivery man, counsel you in preparation of your arrival here?"

Junie nodded favorably. "Yes, sir, I will confirm that he did."

"Yet, I know he didn't tell you what words to use because he selects lingo from the wrong branch of the service every single time, the dolt! But enter, and let's relieve you of those vittles at once. MEN!" he shouted over his shoulder. "Chow time! Step lively! Gastric delights await! Tell Nedrick front and center with the dough!" He looked up at her and used his forehead as a pointer. He calmed somewhat, smiling at her. "To the kitchen, first mate."

Junie smiled broadly. She felt the situation nearly surreal. "Aye, aye, sir!"

"Excellent!" he declared, and he sounded the horn again. "Instant promotion to the rank of ensign approved, fine young delivery person!"

She laughed as they went in, and her greeter acknowledged what she was carrying in front of her upper torso. "The 'Uncle' did himself proud with my garlic and Italian sausage pizza, I assume? I'm hankering for an ulcer blaster of the first order, Ensign. The pie of last month was a bit on the tame side, though I couldn't complain since Gregory the Dolt was twenty-seven seconds late and I got it for nothing."

Junie had to stop her progress. Knowing the menu so well, she knew of the asterisk listed after the description of this specific offering. It was not for the faint of heart, as she made sure to inform every prospective consumer. "The garlic special is for *you*, sir?"

He halted with her and frowned. "For that, I give myself

a toot! I take it you're experienced with the garlic specials, Ensign?"

"I most certainly am!" she replied with honesty. "Upon my first night of hire at Uncle Tony's, I had a leftover slice. It was cold and not very fresh, but I was afraid to exhale for a full day afterward. I just signaled to everyone that I had laryngitis. I'm sure a garlic smell wafted out of my pores. Do you eat the entire thing yourself?"

"In one sitting, and it's a large pie, if I need remind you," he spoke with great pride.

"Then may I give *you* a toot, sir?"

"By all means, Ensign! Hurl that sucker if you so desire!"

Junie cautiously rebalanced the boxes and reached down to make a fairly decent noise. It seemed to echo in the grand foyer.

The older man before her was impressed and had to state as much. "Young lady, I declare you the finest young delivery person we've ever had on these fair premises! Let's continue our course to the galley. Nedrick seems to be amiss of his duty, but I'm going to let it slide this time. I'm enjoying myself at the moment, and I don't want that downer of a stuffed shirt gumming up the works." He went ahead of her to hold open a swinging door that allowed them passage into the next room.

The simple, soft white and grey tile of the kitchen was a pleasant contrast to the woods of the foyer and sparsely furnished breakfast room they had passed through. The maples and oaks before were dark and detailed, and now the shining steel appliances and basic colors of the large work area made any effort here a reward. The two outside walls of the spacious room were all windows, with a good portion of the back wall lined with rows of herbs. Beyond the panes lay what had to be, as told by her gasp, the most beautiful garden she had ever seen. Rising from it was a large gazebo; its ginger-breaded trim abundantly lined with deep pink roses on lush vines.

"If you would be so good as to put the boxes on the table, Ensign...?" he asked, bringing her back to reality.

Junie turned to him and smiled. "Smith," she answered. "Junie Smith, sir." The five boxes were lowered, and she stood before him with friendship. She took the ticket from her belt and held it with one hand as she expected him to introduce himself with either a handshake, or even a military salute should he be so motivated.

For the past minute, the patron about to dine on Uncle Tony's cuisine had been watching her with a keen interest. He began to smile brightly, pleased and confident in the company he was keeping. "Ensign Junie Smith, may I thoroughly apologize for my lack of civility? I am Admiral Robert Adam Crimmins, retired, of the United States Navy. I am totally at your service, my dear."

Junie smiled, taking his outstretched hand, and laughed when he kissed the back of it. "Is that what you do to all the ensigns, Admiral Crimmins?" she asked, feeling flattered.

"Quite naturally, no, but this is the main benefit of being retired and just turning seventy years young." He patted the "Seventy Rules" over his chest. "I get the opportunity to play senile when it's handy, and I always get away with it. May I inquire if you are an ensign in the singular or plural, without being rude, Smitty?"

Junie didn't mind. She had felt comfortable with him since his first word. "In civilian terms, I am a Miss, Admiral."

"Though it's a gross oversight on the world's part, that's

good news for me! Top notch, I say!" He tooted joyously and kissed her hand again. She laughed. When releasing it, he said "I see you like our quarters, Ensign Smith?"

She smiled and sighed. "Very much, sir. The house and grounds are breathtaking. I should feel overwhelmed by being in such a lovely space, but it's very comfortable and inviting here."

Admiral Crimmins nodded, bringing his chair to turn in the same direction as her gaze. She had scanned the kitchen again, and was now looking out to the garden. He explained to her: "The kitchen is of Lieutenant Harvey's design. Any restaurant in the world would go to extreme maneuvers to have him aboard, but I got him. He was my personal assignment during my years at sea, to my great fortune and preservation.

"The gardens are the doings of Major Downs' green thumbs. Not part of his stint in the army, of course, but his hobby has turned our humble address into a showcase. It attracts not only every bee on the face of the globe, but a few high-brow garden types, too. Keeps away the arthritis, he says, but I say it's the manure he's always carting around!

"The house itself was a hoot, Ensign Junie Whatever Smith...?" he prompted.

"Bernice," she supplied without interrupting his rhythm. She received another tooting for it.

"First class choice of names, Ensign Junie Bernice Smith! Yes, the old headquarters here were a kick in the can, to be forthright. I bought it years before I retired, and you'd never know the shape it was in. Condemned, it was. God forsaken chickens were living in it! A sad and sorry sight, and I didn't even get a respectable egg out of the entire fiasco. Laid things the size of sparrow poop, they did, and you had to take a jackhammer to get past the shell. If you wanted an omelet made with ten thousand eggs, those were the ones to gather, though it more than likely wouldn't be edible, I'm sure. I tell visitors I kept the ugly things and put them in the driveway.

"The town was going to raze the place, and I can't say I even know what possessed me to make such an awful investment. I owned it for years, not even keeping abreast of its condition, but always meaning to do something with it if only because I didn't want to admit I'd made such a dreadful mistake.

"It wasn't until I started collecting other retiring old coot bachelors that things took shape. When Harvey decided to be pensioned off, I put him in charge of the kitchen detail. Downs was already here with his seeds. And they kept their old admiral in mind throughout the whole refurbishing mess, as you can see. All the first floor and outdoors are completely accessible to me and my spokes. Thoughtful men, Harvey and Downs. Glad I met them, indeed. Why, Harvey and I go way back to…well, probably the War of 1812, I don't know, but it was a time of combat, Smits, and my other cook had been shot out from under me. I did it myself, I'll confess to you now! He made the most insufferable blueberry flapjacks I'd ever tasted, so I had every right, as any court in this great country would agree." He looked up at her and winked, waiting.

Junie understood his jest, and she laughed. The admiral liked her wit, and gave her a soft toot before continuing.

"That's when Harvey came aboard, and no one's been in my kitchen since. Quite the travels we had while employed by Uncle Sam. Remind me sometime to tell you about the first dish he ever made for me. It was so awful I tried to throw him overboard! There I was, holding that skinny little runt by one ankle over the side of the tub. My legs worked fine back then, of course, or I couldn't try to invite you to my suite later and impress you with my bars. Too bad you're on duty, wouldn't you say, Smitty?"

"Oh, yes, sir!" Junie laughed. The admiral was in full swing, and she was enjoying it so much, time didn't seem to be passing.

"As for Major Downs, I don't remember when I met that rascal. What a bug he used to be! Always up to his neck in it. Gave the MP's their share of grey, I'm sure. But once they ironed him out, he was of the first order. Handsome devil in his time. Probably how he got away with so much! Those roses you see out there are his own breed. Yes, I say, his own breed—registered with his name and all. I don't particularly want to know how a male human creates a pink rose, but since the thing is so beautiful, we won't press the matter.

"Harrison—the one odd-ball who wanted the plain pie you brought there—is a horse of a different color. Quiet as a church mouse, he is. He's a painter now, but he started off as a fly-boy in the air force. Broke just about every record they ever had. He's only a handful of years younger than me. I wonder how I met him. Maybe we were competing for the same girl; it's entirely possible at those USO shindigs. Yes, I'll give him credit and say we broke each other's nose over a cow or two just to mix things up. Good thing he's a colonel, or I'd really have him. But there's no disputing he's the best amateur painter I've seen in all my days. Gave him carte blanche for the interior from fore to aft. No two rooms the same, and all better than what you'd fine in a magazine.

"Last and not least is the gimp known as Captain Nedrick. It's understood it's his job, Smits, to keep me in line. We consider him the legal mind of our constituency. He's the youngster, though he thinks it's a sin to act it. Great mind, always knows what to do, but the most bum internals! Too busy to nurse as a lad, maybe, and besides causing his poor mother double congealment, now the boy's laid up with complete failures for hip and knee bones! Had to take an early dive. I'm referring to a medical retirement, Smitty, sadly enough. Born into the Corps, he was in dress uniform before a diaper, though I'm sure marines burst out able to march to the bathroom! Had one hip replaced two months ago and got some bionic thing-or-other installed, I understand. Got to have the other done, too, if he ever heals himself from this one. Then it's the knees. No patience, that's the problem. He expects results *pronto!* It's frustrated the tarnation out of him. He wanted to make a career out of the Corps, quite naturally, and was rising to the top. Just goes to show you, you never know what's coming around next! One hour you're delivering pizzas, the next hour you're being swept off your feet by a---"

"Old wind bag of an admiral," came a voice that startled them both. They had forgotten they were awaiting this presence.

Admiral Crimmins smiled as he turned around. "Nedrick! High time, boy, I was going to charge you with AWOL. I'm pleased to present Miss Junie Bernice Smith, whom I've already promoted to the rank of ensign. She's the top dog of garlic special deliverers. I was just about to torture a confession out of her concerning the whereabouts of Gregory The Dolt, our usual fine, young delivery man. Five will get you ten that she's bopped old Greg on the noggin and stuffed his body in the trunk of her vehicle out there! We retired coots have no idea how competitive delivery routes can be, and she has every mark of being deviously ruthless, wouldn't you say? Pay her right away or she'll take out the lanyard she's got in that apron thing and string you up with it. She's going to hide out with me, so I'm safe."

Junie was giggling. She lightly touched her fingertips to one of the admiral's expressive cheeks. "Sir, if you are anything derogatory, it's not boring!"

He, in turn, used his horn with more gusto than before. "Ensign Junie Bernice Smith, make me an honest man and marry me! I don't know if I still have the power to perform the ceremony myself, but I'm sure the Good Lord will dance at our wedding!"

Captain Nedrick stepped forward and sternly eyeballed his elated friend. The 'boy' was a slender man approaching forty years of age, who carried a thick black cane he leaned upon heavily. His smile, when it happened, was toothy and he wasn't notably handsome, but he had a deliberate manner about him that said he was more than capable of handling a number of feisty officers, though this one he was quite fond of. His eyes were grey and his hair dark brown, and in contrast to the casual dress of the admiral, he wore shined shoes, belted slacks, and a long-sleeved shirt with a tie held in place by his branch's clasp. Junie agreed he did look more mature and bureaucratic than necessary.

"At the risk of putting a damper on things, I would like to remind Miss Smith that she still has to collect and return a payment," he pointed out.

Both Admiral Crimmins and Junie found the verbal memo saddening. "I told you he was stuffed shirt. Don't you believe in shore leaves, boy? No toot for some time for you. I could have been on my honeymoon tonight!"

She couldn't have him depressed. "I'll bring my veil with the next garlic special, Admiral," she said, passing the charge slip to the captain.

Her effort was successful, and the admiral was overjoyed once more. "I *like* this girl, Nedrick! Like her very much! She's due for *big things*, I tell you! I knew the minute I laid eyes on her! No, the *second* I heard her voice at that intercom-jiggy! It's kismet, or whatever the word is! Smits, tell Uncle Tony to start making my next pie!"

The captain sked him. He had read the order slip. "Admiral, you ordered a garlic special? No offense, Miss Smith, but we've had a thorough discussion with him about this. All hands on deck to open the windows before that box is touched. If it's possible to eat outside tonight, may I suggest it in the most adamant terms, sir?"

The admiral only nodded in agreement as he looked at Junie. "Cleaned me plumb out, it did, but who knows if I didn't get another five years to live because of it? I haven't used the motorized chair since! This one might have me walking again!"

Junie laughed, accepting the bills from the captain. It was past time to depart, and the men began escorting her to the front entry. "If you do get to your feet, Admiral, Tony is looking for a busboy. I'll put in a good word for you. The biggest perk is free food. You could have one of those every night, if you wanted." She giggled.

Admiral Crimmins chuckled as he wheeled along. They slowed their former pace to accommodate the captain. "Tell him to expect my résumé by nine bells, Ensign Smith! I am with earnest hopes that I qualify!"

Junie smiled at the captain and offered her hand. "It was nice to meet you, sir." She then leaned down and gave the admiral a kiss on his cheek. "Happy Belated Birthday, Admiral. And many, many more. Enjoy your pizzas, and don't forget about the windows or the busboy job, sir!"

The horn sounded magnificently. "Smitty, my heart is in shambles! You *must* come back soon! Promise me that, *please!"*

"Enemy waters couldn't keep me away! Thank you! Good bye!"

Junie laughed and waved to them as she rounded her car to the driver's side. Captain Nedrick had dismissed her and departed, and the admiral had saluted and was about to shut the door. When she glanced down to reach for the handle, she gasped. Her good mood changed drastically.

"Oh, no! Oooooh, no." She winced heavily and brought a palm to the side of her face. "Oh, not again. That *is* my spare!" She had to sigh sadly as she realized the economic disaster this was. "Just when I was about to get ahead for a change." She stood and stared at a tire that was flatter than any she had seen before. Tears stung her eyes as a momentary feeling of defeat and shame gripped her.

Being severely short-sighted, Admiral Crimmins was unable to see beyond where she was standing, but he could hear her well enough and the tone of her voice distressed him. "Ensign? Is there trouble in the ranks? What is it, dear? Gregory The Dolt hasn't resuscitated himself and brought the authorities, has he?" Though lined with mirth, his voice was gentle as he attempted to cheer her.

She sighed. "No, I have a flat tire, sir. A *very* flat tire."

"Ahh," he spoke, more optimistic now. "Damsel in distress! Damsel in distress!" he called over both shoulders. "Alert, men, alert! Inner tube incident at one o'clock! All hands to battle stations! This is not a drill. I repeat, this is not a drill!" He returned to roll along the entryway sidewalk, sympathetic about the situation. "We'll fix you up straight away, my dear. There are three able-bodies among us; one of them has to remember what to do. We've seen plenty of horrific action between us, Smits; this certainly ought to be something we can handle."

She was shaking her head as Captain Nedrick reappeared, and three other men she had heard of, yet not met, began to assemble behind him. Her voice was forlorn. "No, sir, there's nothing you can do. I'm so sorry this had to happen here, but I should have known, I guess. I can change tires myself, but the one that's flat is the spare. The other tire burst last week and I haven't had the time to fix it. If I could just use your phone to call the restaurant, that will be all I ask. I'll get a garage, or something, to take care of it." She looked at the offending wheel and closed her eyes, not knowing where the funds would come from to ensure that.

The admiral was not satisfied with this strategy. "Men, there's nothing else to do but give her a loner, what do you say?"

Captain Nedrick was more restrained, and he spoke for all of them. This appeared to be commonplace, for they all looked to him before any words had been uttered. "Admiral, forgive me, but I think the wiser action would be for one of us to drive Miss Smith to the restaurant. She can make arrangements from there, with no rush on our part for her vehicle remaining here. Excuse me, Miss Smith, I mean no disrespect, but I'm sure you understand."

Junie was nodding with embarrassment. "A ride is even too much! Tony or Alberto will come to get me. Please, Admiral, just a phone call is enough. I won't accept anything more. Thank you very much, but I must refuse your generous offer."

"Now see here!" He slapped the padded arm of his chair. His ability to command came to the forefront. "I am the highest ranking officer of this outfit! I was promoted to this level because I had unfailingly exhibited outstanding judgment in times where instantaneous decisions concerning many lives and millions of dollars in property were on the line. Do you honestly think I have come so far only to blow a situation as simple as this? What are you people thinking?" He turned to one of the men behind him. "Harvey, you know where my keys are. Ensign Smith will be acquisitioned my car. Bring it around *at once*, and I will not hear any guff about it. Go on, I say. Go on."

The lieutenant only quickly glanced at the tight-lipped captain, then stepped from the group and passed her for the garages.

"Not a word from you, boy," the admiral knew to say under his breath. He then returned his smile to Junie.

"Smitty, I wish I were doing you more of a favor, but I believe the only reason Captain Stuffed Shirt here isn't putting up more of an argument is because my horseless carriage is probably a grandparent to what you drove onto the premises. It's an automatic transmission, though, and once she gets warmed up, she'll run well.

"When Harvey brings her around, off you go to your workplace, and by the time you get there, I will have spoken to the Uncle and apprised him of the situation. If you experience anything less than unadulterated understanding from your employer, I want to know about it before the hour is out. You will make your appointed rounds and keep this car until arrangements for new tires have been made, is that clear? When all is well with your job and your ride again, you return the old gal to me and maybe in payment you'll dine with me one night. How does that sound, dear? Have I come to the rescue more than enough? I want to see you happy again." He waited, requiring her bright smile as his answer.

Junie took one of his hands, though a red color tinged her face. "You have, Admiral, and I'm very, very grateful. It's not much, I know, but I need this job. I'll have your car back to you not only cleaned and polished, but dinner will be on me, if you can stand cooking other than Lieutenant Harvey's." She tried to grin, but could only bend to kiss his cheek again, giving him an embrace. She had been struggling with her financial circumstances for so long; she had begun to feel she would never escape the drudgery of having to work so many positions just to afford getting by. Tears filled her eyes for his kindness to a relative stranger.

"It's settled, then. I'll see you in a few days, Ensign Junie!" He tooted his horn, the car was brought alongside hers, and Lieutenant Harvey held open the door for her.

"Thank you. Thank you so much. Captain Nedrick, I promise I won't disappoint you." Junie quivered as she sank into the velvety leather seat. She put the beautiful car in gear, and the gates yawned for her exit. The electric window descended silently, and she waved until out of sight.

"Quiet in the ranks," the admiral said as all left him but a displeased captain. "The starch in your shirt is aging you terribly, boy. More than your hips and knees need to be replaced, by the looks of it. A pretty young thing needing aid and all you think of is an old jalopy?"

Captain Nedrick exhaled loudly, shaking his head. "The 'old jalopy' is a classic luxury vehicle of which only five hundred were made thirty years ago, and it's so costly to insure and maintain, it's been parked in the garage for the past ten years. Except for a slow spin around the property, even you won't allow it on the street. You won't see that particular means of transportation again, Admiral. Don't be eyeballing me when you're filling out a stolen vehicle report in a few days, sir."

"Ah, you know better yourself or you wouldn't have stood for it. There's no silver spoon in her mouth, I'll agree with that, but that's not pyrite in her heart. She's got gumption, she does, and I like it! Now, off to the phone with me so I can speak to the Uncle before she gets there. Out of the way, you honeymoon wrecker, you!"

Captain Nedrick put a hand on one hip, but reluctantly half-grinned as he watched him spin away.

Junie wanted to make several detours with the car, yet felt it dishonest. She had smiled so thoroughly while driving the perfect machine that her face actually hurt, but now as she parked near the restaurant door, her smile left her. Tony, Alberto, and even Greg were waiting and watching for her. Tony himself opened the eatery door for her.

"Junie! I did not know! Come in, come in! Are you tired? Have a seat! Greg, you idiot, give her your stool!"

"I get you a drink, Junie! I know what you like!" Off ran Alberto.

Instead of being incensed, Greg hobbled around the best he could. "Here, Junes. Man alive! I didn't know you knew how to do that stuff! You're cooler than I thought! *And do you have any idea what you're driving?* My auto shop teacher would *die!*"

Tony slapped his hands to his flushed cheeks, not thinking about the automobile first. His eyes rolled in a great circle. "Too bad this can't be in the papers! This would be great advertise for us, but I make sure everyone know! People will come to eat because they know they are so safe here! Junie! Good girl! Sit! Sit! What do you want! Rest you arms. Rest you wonderful arms!" He nearly embraced her, forcing her to relax.

A stunned Junie glanced at Greg as she took the soda from Alberto. "My arms? But all I did was---"

"Ha! Listen to her! All you did was save that poor man's life! This is nothing? It is something! He should kiss you, he should! He should kiss you feet! I watch the shows on TV! The hugging thing you do, and pop! Out come the stuck food. My garlic special, nearly too much for him this time, but not when you there! Pop! Out comes my beautiful crust. We make sure when we tell this story it's not the pizza fault, but that he was so hungry he couldn't chew it right. Now he lives, he breathes, and he still eat my pizza all the time! And look! It's not a made-up pretend story, there is the car! And an Italian car, too, I will cry for such happiness! I should kiss you feet, too!" Antonio did glance at her shoes, but winced at the older sneakers and took her hand instead. "There! I kiss you hand! There! I kiss it again, maybe." He didn't.

Junie was smiling. "This seems to be the day for it," she whispered to herself. "Thank you, Admiral." She laughed.

Section Two: The Contact

[THREE DAYS LATER; 16:00 HOURS]

During the time Junie used the admiral's car, she learned to hum in a pitch harmonious to the purring engine. She lovingly hand-washed the auto, vacuumed away the fine layer of interior dust, and filled the tank with premium fuel. Admiral Crimmins accepted with delight her date for an early evening dinner, and when coming to the gate this time, it opened without any use of jocularity on either side of the call box.

The retired military man had taken a dress uniform out of storage and sent it to the cleaners. He greeted her on the patio, holding out his arms, and before removing the two grocery bags from the auto's trunk compartment, she clasped his hands and gave him a kiss on the cheek. He had even polished the bicycle horn to a gleaming.

She stood smiling before him, pleasantly dressed in a yellow knit top and a cotton gauze skirt that went just below her knees. Her feet were clad in open-toed sandals, and her hair was brushed plainly and attractively, unbound to her shoulders. Her face was shining and pretty, and her figure trim and healthy. Her understated jewelry and belt were fitting accessories to her.

"For you, my white knight!" Junie said, presenting him with a bouquet of various flowers from one of the bags. "I guess it's silly bringing a man flowers when the garden at his house is far superior, but I have to express my gratitude somehow. You took a small tragedy and turned it into a wonderful week. I don't know how to thank you, sir. And, because I already had the reputation, I learned how to do the Heimlich maneuver."

They both laughed, looking to each other with their growing friendship. "I started out by saying it was the stuffed shirt of an old hobbler, Nedrick, who was stricken, Ensign. Since the boy was right there when I was calling the Uncle, I was going to give him the honor of being the star of the show. But, as he was making my tale difficult to tell by standing to port and shaking his head the entire time, I changed the victim to be yours truly. Clever it was, I tell you, and as you can see, I've fully recovered from the near death experience with the only change being an increased desire to consume garlic specials. I have no doubt had the rest of the house known part of the scenario would include your arms being wrapped tightly about them, they would have attempted eating their entire meal in one bite, causing mass asphyxiation. Half of our number would have perished gruesomely, but the other half would know sheer bliss. It would be worth it! I just may fake something else tonight to take the chance you'll revive me. Take your time, my dear, and if any of those old coots in there try to push you aside to help, I give you permission to shoot them without asking questions! What are my chances, Smitty? Give it to me straight—I'm an old seadog and can take it. It doesn't much matter, I'll just keep collapsing until something works, I dare say."

Junie was laughing, and they headed over the marble floor of the foyer and the parquet tile of the breakfast room to enter the kitchen. She held the doors open for him this time. "You'll be eating my cooking, Admiral Crimmins. That might do you in before you have the chance to fake anything!"

He tooted the horn, openly merry for her company. Junie was very comfortable with him as well, and she began taking out the ingredients for their dinner and putting them on the island, or in the refrigerator behind her.

"I have one special dish, so if you want to have more than one meal that I cook, I'm in trouble! I can boast only about my barbecued chicken. I make my own sauce. I know you like spicy food, so I bought extra cayenne, sir. I brought my little hibachi, too, and I thought I'd take it somewhere outside, away from the garden in case the smoke hurts Major Downs' beautiful flowers, and we'll grill. I also brought some fresh peas to steam. We can shell them together, if you'd like, Admiral. Do you like peas, sir?"

He nodded firmly, but frowned at the same time. "In all honesty, Ensign Junie, I detest all forms and figures of vegetables, but from your hand I would eat what Downs' fertilizes his garden with. Don't rat on me to Harvey, though. That would diminish my power over him! He still submits his menus for my approval, and he shakes when he sees my mere eyebrow rise! We have sour cream. Always a hearty stock of it. Drown anything questionable with the stuff, that's my motto. I'll eat just about anything that way. Harvey discovered that secret long ago. Don't know exactly what I've eaten over the years, to tell you the truth, but I'm not dead yet. If it's covered in sour cream, I don't ask. I just say 'Tasty looking vittles once again, haven't we, Harvey?' and dig in."

Junie had to be amused. "Your diet is as amazing as you are, sir!"

"Ah, that's the perk of a long military career, my dear. They use scrap metal in the stuff they feed you in basic. We were luckier than the slobs in the army. They ate boots. We had old ships. Saves the taxpayers millions, I'm sure. No iron-poor blood in my branch! You didn't pass basic unless your urine was rusty and your stool had five links from an anchor chain in it. I imagine Downs had fighter planes and Nedrick had, well, old hairy drill sergeants in full battle gear, I suppose. From my observation, there are only two things marines ever truly love, and that's their country and their mama. Strictly in that order, too, with the mama sometimes being optional. Indeed, I've witnessed it myself, if they fall and scrape their knees, they bellow for Uncle Sam first! The rest is second rate, no matter what it is.

"And speaking of old coots, I took the liberty of having them set us up a table in the gazebo, dear. It's a beautiful night in our fair state of Virginia, and with the moth ball smell I've got fumigating the entire place, the bees should scram. Pass me whatever supplies you need, and we'll go shell the detestable peas out there. It will also give the magpies their divine opportunity to spy on us. I know they're just dying to see what goes on." His laugh had a delightedly mischievous lilt to it.

There was a large pot rack above the workspace, and she stopped her removal of what she thought they'd require. "Sir, your house mates? They want to spy on us?"

He tooted the horn. "Quite naturally! I expect it, Smitty, would even demand it! Feed from Intelligence is life's blood among the upper ranks, even if we have to gather it ourselves. It's good for them, really—should take some of the cobwebs from between their retired toes! And since I entertain someone of your ilk once every two thousand years, they'd just better do it or I'll be gravely insulted! If I weren't so fortunate as to be your host tonight, Ensign, I'd have my nose pressed to the glass as well."

"Oh, my," Junie commented with a quick giggle.

"Harrison has a pair of field specs he keeps on that upper shelf. Downs' blooms attract a plethora of birds, and Harrison likes the humming varieties in particular. Harvey removed the specs today and was adjusting them. We'll have to give the old biddies a show, what do you say? We'll think up something good. Get those arms in shape, Ensign; we may need all their brawn tonight!"

He chuckled, and took the saucepans, colander, and bag of peas from her and put them in his lap. "Out to the gardens, my dear. I guarantee you before we hit the wood of the gazebo floor, the school marms will be accumulating!"

Junie laughed. She looked over his shoulder as she grasped the handles of his chair to power him out the opened French doors to a slate walkway. The kitchen became quiet, but not for long.

Alan Downs had been given two choices when he was eighteen: Join the armed services for a four year stint, or go to prison for attempted car theft, which capped a career of petty crimes. The youth with the hardened attitude swore to break the will of the army, but instead he fell in love with his occupation and quickly excelled. During convalescence after a training accident, he discovered gardening, and it further calmed his soul. He was tall, just a bit on the bulky side after retiring five years before, and the black of his hair was becoming doused with gray. He entered the kitchen first; his past still igniting sparks inside him. He went straight to the work island and looked over the bags the young woman he had heard so much about had brought.

Donald Harvey was just the opposite: Much shorter in stature, wide in build, flat of stomach, and had the same color of blonde hair as when he was born. Perhaps the strand count was the same also, but he would never grey.

He had joined the navy because, after trying in almost every other branch, they would bend the height rule for him if he signed for culinary duty. He found his niche and stayed there until his retirement, proud to follow and serve the admiral he so greatly admired. He came into the kitchen next, and went over to his best friend. "What did she bring?" They kept their voices low.

"Nothing extraordinary, yet," Major Downs answered as he poked through the few items. Then he stopped and looked at his partner in the search. "Harri, has retirement come to this?"

The lieutenant shook his head, but made a quick glance out the windows to check on their distance. "If it were you or I having a date, he'd be the first to round the rest up and post us at different angles outside, probably with cameras and microphones, you can bet. What did she bring?"

Downs smiled, knowing he was right. "You're the cook, but it looks like chicken. There are a few tomatoes, and what's this?" He pulled out a glass bottle and was unscrewing the top to sniff it.

"No!" Harvey stopped him in time. "That's cayenne pepper, you fool! You'd sneeze for a month if your nose didn't burn off! Talk about being caught red-handed, it would be all over your face, Rudolph!" He put a hand over his mouth to keep from laughing too hard. He then calmed. "If I didn't know she knew he has a stomach stronger than the *Iowa*, I'd say she was pulling something fishy."

The major turned his gaze from the sacks to the gazebo. "So you think she's got something up her sleeve, too? It's one of the oldest tricks in the book: Get the old geezer to leave you everything in his will, and then bump him off! Saints preserve us!"

The lieutenant narrowed his eyes and leaned over the

counter, staring at the couple outside. Major Downs mimicked him, concentrating as thoroughly. It was more from guilt than a stealthy approach that made the men jump when Colonel Harrison asked in a normal voice:

"What's going on here?"

"Shush!" responded Downs. "Harrison! Do you want to give us away? And you know darned well what's going on. Come here. There she is."

Hezekiah Harrison was the second oldest in the group of five, and the most mild, both in temperament and appearance. He was lanky, appeared very flexible, and had a thatch of dark red hair at the top of his head. Unlike other men who went bald from the top down, he had a ring around the middle of his head with thick hair above and below it. He had retired with a distinguished record from the air force, though his service was done so quietly, it wasn't given the honor it was due. He was the only bashful man of the near half-dozen, and, after Captain Nedrick, often was looked to as the voice of reason. "That's who he was talking about at breakfast today, dinner last night, lunch yesterday, and all those other days before that?"

"That's the one," the lieutenant supplied. "Be quiet."

The three men nearly pressed their shoulders together in order to see out without being seen. The work island was their cover, and they leaned over it to better scrutinize their subjects.

"Darn your flowers, Downs," Harvey said. "I can hardly see a thing. Where's a flame thrower when you need one?"

The other two smiled. "Harri, don't you keep a pair of binoculars in here?" the major inquired. "To watch for your birds, you know? Where the heck are they?"

"Why, I never!" Colonel Harrison said. "You're not going

to use my binoculars for a purpose like---"

"Here, Downs. I dusted them off this morning after I did the dishes. Why didn't you bring your own pair?"

"Well, to tell you the truth…" He handed Harrison's pair back to Harvey and pulled a smaller size from his trouser pocket. They looked at each other and laughed.

"You both should be ashamed! I should inform Admiral Crimmins at once!" the colonel sputtered.

"Oh, put a sock in hit, Harrison," said Downs. "Suppose you tell us why you've come to the kitchen at this precise time?"

"Well, I…"

Lieutenant Harvey laughed and nudged him with an elbow. "You're curious too, Harrison, admit it!"

He scratched his head, but more to stall his answer than to think. "All right, so I want to know about her. The admiral is quite taken with her. I didn't get that close a look at her the other day. I want to see what all the fuss is about."

Downs and Harvey put their elbows on the work surface and began adjusting the lenses. "I never thought I'd say this, but darn my own flowers! I've given them quite a romantic setting, too. It should be impossible for any self-respecting woman to refuse an advance in that atmosphere, if I do say so myself."

The lieutenant chortled. "He asked me today if I thought he looked better with his glasses off. He was turned to the closet door at the time, and he thought it was me! If he does make a pass at her, it would ruin the entire effect if he did it in the wrong direction."

Even Colonel Harrison had to smile at that, and he leaned over the counter with them once more.

"Hello, girls," came the fourth voice.

Harrison corrected his posture with humiliation. "Why,

Captain! Isn't it fortuitous that you should join us at this time? We were about to get something to drink, weren't we, men?"

"What's the matter, Neddie? Can't see them from your room, either?" the major asked.

Nedrick stood still for a moment, and then gave in. "Darn you and your flowers, Downs. Why couldn't you come up with the miniature size?" Perhaps more honest than the rest, his binoculars were openly hanging from his neck. He came up beside the colonel and took his position over the counter. The four of them stood side by side. "At least I have the excuse of surveillance to protect the admiral's best interests. You ladies just want to gossip. So, let's have it, gals. Has anything happened?"

"We can just make them out. You don't have a flame thrower, do you, Cappy?" Lieutenant Harvey wanted to know.

"Fresh out."

"Then we're out of luck."

"Tell me about her," Harrison asked. "I have a spare pair of field glasses in my room, but I'd probably miss the whole thing. What does she look like?"

Captain Nedrick paused his viewing to turn to him. "You saw her the other day, Harrison. Didn't you look?"

The elder man shook his head. "I came in only to get my pizza when I heard the admiral yell about her flat tire. When he said he was going to give her the car and you didn't protest, I just got my food and left. You were standing beside me, Downs. What is she like?"

He cleared his throat. "Well, I didn't really pay too much attention. I couldn't, actually. Harvey was in the way."

The other three laughed. "That's a good excuse," Nedrick

pointed out. "He's only about three feet shorter than the rest of us."

"I am not!"

"Shhhh!" They chuckled.

"You were right next to her, Harvey, when she got in the car. What does she look like?" the colonel still tried.

"I swear, Downs, I'm going to chop down every single one of those blasted flowers! I never did like them, and I'm allergic to bee stings! Well…she's a few inches taller than me."

"How unusual!" the major teased.

Harvey nudged him. "And that's about it. It was hard to tell. She…well, she had on a uniform."

"A uniform? She was delivering pizzas!" the captain interjected. "Is this what happens with retirement? She probably only had on jeans and a tee shirt."

"Wait a minute here, *you* tell us about her, Neddie Boy! *You* talked with her, and *you* paid her, for crying out loud! What is she like? How are her looks?" Downs insisted.

Nedrick took a deep breath, and then firmly went with: "It was impossible to tell. She had on the ugliest baseball cap I've ever seen. That threw me off."

Muted laughter came from the other three. "Saints preserve us!" Major Downs decided. "We'd have lost every single skirmish if not for regulation gear! How many men did we misplace that were on R and R?"

The captain had to smile.

"Well, you all have glasses now," Harrison said, "And I don't. Describe her to me. Tell me what they're doing."

They all took as close a study as they could.

"Looks like she has long, black hair," Downs reported.

"She does not," commented Harvey. "That's a shadow. It's short and light colored. It's very curly."

"It's more Harrison's shade. Harvey, it's as straight as an arrow. Where did she put it the other day? Under her ugly cap? I would have sworn she was nearly bald," Nedrick retorted.

"I don't really care about the hair. Is she clean looking? I want her to be an all-American, lovely, girl-next-door type," the colonel attempted with a sweet grin.

"I don't think you'd be pleased, Harri. She's got on pancake make-up. Coats and coats of it," the major chimed in. "I can see the pock marks from here." He winced. "I think some of them are moving."

"Downs, will you take into account the shade from your flowers and that maybe there are a few insects out there? Pock marks don't move! Looking at her like that, she's got holes the size of dessert plates everywhere! I hope she's got *some* paint on. The admiral's wearing his whites. We can look for smudges." Harvey laughed, though somewhat shyly.

Nedrick was scowling. "What's that green stuff they're tossing around out there?"

"I think it's corn. They're shucking corn," Downs said. "They're tossing it at each other."

"I hope not. The admiral bruises easily," commented Harrison.

"They're not tossing it at each other! They're shelling peas. Good grief," related the chef.

Colonel Harrison was exasperated. "I don't care about the 'green stuff', anyway. What about the rest of her? What is she wearing? How is her figure? Is she graceful or clumsy, what is she doing, can you at least tell me that much!"

"*Shhhhh!*"

"Darn it, Harrison, I'd have you look for yourself, but I'm

mad at you now!" the lieutenant said. No one else offered.

"She's got on a short-sleeved—"

"No, it's long-sleeved."

"Blouse."

"I think she has on a skirt."

"Those are loose dress slacks."

"It's a pretty floral print."

"It's checkered."

"Is that a belt around her waist, or a snake?"

They laughed.

"I can't see her feet."

"Oh, what does it matter? We haven't exactly done too well with the rest of her."

Laughter sounded again.

"She's most definitely on the plump side."

"She's underweight. No doubt about it."

"Girls, all we can swear to is that she's blurry."

There were more chuckles, but they had to agree with Captain Nedrick. None of them could focus properly.

"What are they doing?"

"It looks like they're eating the corn, raw."

"It's *peas*, and it doesn't matter what vegetable it is. The admiral won't eat it unless he brought sour cream out there."

The captain made a disgusted noise and passed his glasses to the colonel. "Here, Harrison, give it a shot. I think we've all failed this exercise. It's clear our specs are made for greater distances. They can't be any more than twenty yards from us, and we're as blind as bats. Good thing we're not under attack." He brought his cane around and corrected his posture.

Harrison pursed his lips. "You're right, as usual, Captain. We can't tell. These glasses were made for…!"

Three grown men made a terrible inhaling sound at the same time.

"What?" Nedrick asked with alarm.

"She can see us! *Incoming!*"

The mature officers, some with high ranks, crouched down as quickly as possible and protected themselves as if expecting a bomb.

Junie laughed. "Admiral, there were four men standing at the kitchen island. Three of them had binoculars. They don't realize it, but the ceiling lights are on over the work island, and the light reflected on the lenses as if they were holding up flashlights!" She laughed.

"What are they doing now, dear?" he asked calmly, putting a few peas in the colander. His back was toward them.

"I think they saw me look over and they ducked down behind the counter." Her laugh grew, and he smiled with her.

"We have several options, Ensign. One, would you like to do a strip-tease?"

She smiled at him. "No, sir."

"How about a long, drooly smooch?"

"Not this soon," she answered with mirth.

He had to toot the horn for that. "Would you like to sit in my lap?"

"Negative, sir."

"How about if I sit in your lap?"

Junie laughed anew.

"Then there's only one thing to do. Take the bull by the horns, Ensign! Don't beat around the bush! Get straight to the matter! Cut to the chase! When they stand up again and think themselves safe, wave as big as a pompous politician!

We'll go into the kitchen and I'll introduce you to the magpies, if you still care to meet them."

She sounded her agreement by laughing, and she didn't have to wait long. "Are you ready, Admiral Crimmins?"

"Yes, my dear. Fire in the hole!"

Junie stood and looked directly into the kitchen and waved heartedly.

"We've been had!"

"Direct hit!"

"I'm so ashamed!"

The captain laughed. "What?"

"We should have known the old fox would suspect!" Major Downs declared. "They're coming! Ditch the glasses!"

Nedrick shook his head. "No doubt he knows that, too. He was probably counting on it." Yet, Downs and Harvey each opened any drawer they could and slammed them shut with the field glasses inside.

"Here they come!" Colonel Harrison whispered, nearly dropping Nedrick's binoculars on the floor in front of his feet. Junie came in, pushing the admiral in front of her. Her eyes were twinkling with the teasing she and her dinner partner were enjoying.

Nervously, three men cleared their throats, and one straightened his tie. "Good evening, sir!" they greeted. "Good evening, Miss Smith."

"Hello!"

"Smitty, meet the old maids of the quilting bee," Admiral Crimmins called out. He asked her to stand beside him. The men came from around the counter like young children expecting their deserved discipline, with Harrison kicking over the binoculars on the way. They stood erect, as if still on active duty, looking off over the heads of those before them.

"This is Major Alan Taft Downs, retired, of the United States Army. Our illustrious gardener. He's fifty-nine years young, and is probably kicking himself for encouraging such full blooms in the way of his range of vision. Better luck next time, eh, Downs? You did not detail the gazebo for surveillance, are you finding, lad? It's made you a bit unpopular at the moment, I suspect."

He was nearly as pink as his namesake blooms. "Yes, sir. I'm sorry, sir. Hello, Miss Smith. It's nice to see you again," he murmured, clearly suffering.

"Hello, Major Downs. I've never been in such a beautiful garden. Congratulations on having a rose named after yourself. Please leave them the size that they are, because they're gorgeous," Junie spoke with as much kindness as possible.

"Thank you very much, Miss Smith." He wanted to slink away.

"This is Lieutenant Donald Lee Harvey, retired, of the United States Navy. My second favorite cook, now. He is a year younger than Downs, but so much smarter and righteous, I'm sure he just walked into the kitchen and was vehemently protesting this rude behavior, knowing how it might insult a lady and infuriate me, right, son? Meet Junie Smith, Lieutenant Lucifer Harvey."

He inhaled deeply. "Miss Smith, it is an honor to meet you."

Junie wished they would look at her so they would know she was far from being upset. "Hello, Lieutenant. Thank you. I'm hoping my cooking will pass without too much sour cream tonight."

"I'm sure it will, Miss. Thank you." He swallowed loudly, and apparently with pain.

"And what do know, there's my old friend, Colonel Hezekiah Leslie Harrison, our resident artist! He retired a few years after me from the United States Air Force, and now, at the tender age of sixty-seven years, he's launched himself upon a new career of becoming a peeping tom! How is it going, Harrison? Any deviant peeps you'd like to share with the superior officer you were practicing upon?"

The colonel felt himself burning with humiliation, and the admiral knew this sensitive man, and his oldest friend, would feel his comments more than the others.

"Miss Smith, I offer my most profound apologies, and may I also say that if I ever took up the pastime the admiral stated, though you would make a fine subject, I would never consider peeping upon you."

The only break in the men's composures came here when just their eyes stole toward the befuddled speaker of the humorous sentence.

Junie smiled warmly, holding her mirth. "Thank you, Colonel. I'm flattered you think me as peep upon-ish. I'm very glad to meet you, sir."

"Thank you, Miss Smith. Thank you very much!" He nearly bowed.

"And Captain H. Rodgers Nedrick, the stuffiest shirt of the lot, you've met. Thirty-seven he is, Smits, but add about sixty years, and it is *not* to his credit, as you can plainly see.

"Nedrick, pick up your specs, herd the little kiddies out of this room, and make sure the juvenile population of my house gives me a moment of peace with this outstanding young woman! All of you take the look you were too cowardly to do in a polite way. She is outstanding in beauty, manners, attire and make up, so beg forgiveness and take your leave! And may I never be so embarrassed by my own household again! What, with your retirements—medical or otherwise—have the manners your branches bore into you in hopes you'd become gentlemen, stay behind?

"Perhaps we should take out our manuals and do a little brushing-up instead of playing cards every night! Think it didn't matter anymore? Think you don't have to make your branches or yourselves proud anymore? You had best think again! As long as you use your rank in front of your name, you have a tremendous responsibility! Now, take this lesson to heart, men, and ponder it well as you *attempt* to slumber tonight! Dismissed!"

The captain turned to the men at his right and waited for them to nod to Junie, and retreat in single file. The scolding had been very docile—for Junie's sake, he knew—but the purpose was still there, and he had to agree with it. He carefully retrieved his binoculars, put them around his neck again, and saluted smartly to the admiral.

"Sir, good evening. Miss Smith, good evening. On behalf of my fellow officers, I apologize for our behavior and beg your tolerance. You shall not be reminded of our presence unless we're called upon to be of service in any manner. Good night, sir. Good night, Miss Smith."

Junie was as embarrassed as the other men. "Thank you, Captain Nedrick," she spoke softly with warmth. "I take no offense at all. Please tell the others that I'm very glad to have met them."

"That's very generous of you. Thank you, Miss."

Admiral Crimmins dismissed him with a salute, and the captain departed the room. The door swung silently behind him. After a short pause, a smile burst over his angered expression. "Ah, that was fun, Smits! I don't get to spout off at them very often; I wish I had been more brutal! Did that bother you, dear?"

She playfully cringed, resting a palm on his shoulder. "Do they know it was a joke, or that I'm not mad, sir?"

He patted the back of her hand. "Quite naturally, they do! And you said so yourself. I know them in and out, Ensign, and let me tell you that they're laughing about it already. Come! Get the sour cream, start the coals, and let's keep making headway toward that drooly kiss I've been promised!"

Junie laughed, relaxed again, and the rest of the night went by without giving the incident a second thought. When it was time for her to leave, she found one of the men had brought her car around to the front entry, and four new tires with bright white-walls caught the glow of the lit garden and house. The fountain was illuminated as well, and the splashing and tune from the crickets lent the house a quiet peace. Her kiss was another aimed for the cheek, and the admiral stayed out waving and tooting his horn until the gates were shut.

"Nedrick!" he shouted when locking the front door. "Boy, where are you?"

The captain came from the front parlor where he and the others were enjoying a rubber of bridge, and their nightly drinks and cigars. "Yes, sir?"

"It was a fine night. Charming girl in every which way."

He nodded. "Yes, sir. Admiral, we didn't mean any disrespect. I hope you—"

"Oh, just strutting my stuff, you know, boy, for the ensign. Forget about that. I was good in my time, I'll have you know. I could take the crustiest of seamen and reduce them to tears. Absolute tears, they'd be in! Some never even cried at their mama's funeral, but once they got used to me, out would come the hankies if I only walked by! Loved them all, I did. Never met one I didn't care for. God bless them all.

Nedrick there's something I want you to do for me."

"Yes, sir?"

"Remember the contract? The one you wrote up for me some time ago."

He was surprised. "Yes?"

"Do you still have it, boy?"

"I do, sir…"

"Dig it out. Get it ready. She's coming back for dinner next Monday on her night off. I said we'd put on a show to attempt proving our better qualities. After dinner we'll have ourselves a little chat." He nodded his head with thought.

"Sir? You don't think…"

The admiral looked up at him with a decisive frown. "I *do* think! Uncanny I am about this sort of thing, boy, just uncanny. That's what got me my bars. I'm not one to hold my fire while I'm aimed in the right direction, and it's wartime, my good man! You know me better than that, Rodgers. I could wait, but what for? I don't think this is a thing where getting to know each other better will do the trick, and I'm not decreasing in age, am I? She's top drawer stuff. She'll probably understand even if she thinks I'm worse than anything you men could have done tonight. We'll present it in a delicate fashion, you understand. She's a lady. I knew it right away, like getting hit with lightning, it was! Dig it out, type it up with the proper names, and off we go next week after dinner. Make up a copy for all of us so everyone can read it as we go along. Just maybe—"

"'*All of us*', sir?" the Captain had to protest. His grey eyes rolled justifiably. "You're not going to ask her privately? I don't know if that would be considered delicate, Admiral! I, for one, would feel very awkward!"

Admiral Crimmins waved a hand and frowned. "This is

a simple yes or no business. It's not a thing to brood over! Why pussy-foot around, I'd like to know? I'm not just going to blurt it out. *You're* going to be the one doing that briefing, how else could it be done delicately? So, lose that awkward feeling! You have a week to practice! Use me as a sounding board if need be; what do you say?"

Captain Nedrick inhaled loudly, but he was unable to speak.

"Excellent! I can see the words formulating already. I have every confidence in you! Tell the men full dress, and I'll be conducting an inspection. After all, we'll be entertaining the most important female to ever walk through this door! Good night, boy. I think for the second time in my life, I'm going to dream!"

The captain sighed after he spun away. "Yes, sir." He closed his eyes, but not for rest.

Section Three: The Contract

[FIRST MONDAY IN JUNE; 17:00 HOURS]

They stood in a proud line as if posing for a recruiting poster. Admiral Crimmins brought his wheelchair in front of each one.

"Harvey? Excellent!" he announced, looking over the lieutenant's navy dress uniform. It was complete with hat and gloves. "A sharp looking lad you are, Harvey. Why it is you never married is beyond me. You're not a salty old dog like I am, never were. Got a streak of absolute sentimentality in you, son. Always liked it. Makes you most personable. Good job with the threads tonight." He rewarded him with a toot on the horn.

He saluted. "Sir, thank you!"

"You're welcome. At ease, Lieutenant." He pushed on to Harrison. "Ah, Colonel. Like me, you must have some English lineage in you, my good man. If I didn't know better, I'd say we had the same mum, for you certainly look to have some blue blood in those skinny veins. Where else would you have gotten that dour nose of yours, not that it's a detriment to you, Hezekiah! You are the picture of a proud fly-boy this night. Good job. Jut that chin, my good man, and there's no improving to be done on you."

"Thank you, sir."

The horn had to sound again. "You're quite, quite welcome. As you were. Nedrick! Still using that cane, I see. I don't like it, I don't like it. Can you get your money back, boy? New parts should work better than old ones, and here you are, still tapping along as if you need a boy scout. But, the uniform is above par. If I were in the habit of holding my tongue, I wouldn't tell you that the Corps uniform quite undoes all the rest. Goes well with your color, too. How's that bread basket?" he asked, then managed a clean blow to his stomach.

The captain flinched, not expecting it, and from the shadow of his hat, he frowned down at his friend.

"I'll forgive you this time, but keep dinner light, boy! You have important work to do afterward! You look smashing, son. You might not have to be careful with your words, do you think?" He laughed. "But if she swoons over men in uniform next to you, don't let her near that flabby belly. Look at the men before you, and look at—Downs! What have we here, lad? This is a disaster of the first order!"

The other three broke their stances and had to chuckle. Downs was the exception to the rule. His army dress jacket was straining to the limit to remain closed.

Major Downs cleared his throat with a mirth-filled wince. "Sir, I regret to report that retirement has added a few pounds to my girth. It's Harvey's fault, and yours, too, to be candid, Admiral. I never had much of a taste for sour cream before living here," he spoke at attention.

"But I only use it in extremes, man!"

"Sir, I find many extremes."

"I'll remember that, Downs," Harvey said. They chuckled again.

The admiral was poking the offending visage with a finger. "At ease, son. Are you sucked in?"

He attempted it. "Yes, sir, I am, sir," his voice squealed. The image did not improve.

Admiral Crimmins checked his watch. "If we had the time I'd have you get down and give me two hundred, but

I'm sure that's not the case. The ensign has been prompt every time. She's probably parking as we speak. The only thing to do is to have you remain standing, and behind something at that! You're my barkeep, so that takes care of it out here, and when we go in to dinner, perhaps we can all relax a bit and you can release the poundage. We'll all unbutton, men! That's it, and then the beans won't show! The rest of the time, just don't breathe, is all I can tell you. Gardening is not the exertion you need, man! All those bags of cow dung wasted! It's clearly the pitfall of using the wheelbarrow. Get rid of that contraption, and sling it over your shoulder from now on! And, Harvey, no more sour cream for that man's army! Now, you answer the door when she rings and perhaps you'll lose a particle just moving to-"

The doorbell peeled. The five of them looked to the parlor entry.

"Relax, men! Relax!" Admiral Crimmins nearly cried. "Tonight is going to be perfect! Tonight we're going to wow the lady! Tonight we're going to—where in the blasted configuration of earth is my horn?" He was so nervous, he had missed the bulb altogether.

"Sir, right here," the captain said, guiding the elder man's shaking hand to it.

Admiral Crimmins wailed a single note, and then looked up as if fulfilled. "Nedrick, always there in a pinch, good man. And excellent for the rest of you for keeping your heads, too. We'll get through this and live to brag about it! I've calmed the ranks many times by saying that whether it's been true or not. Let's just have a good time and forget the fact that if I ruin this I'll be the most despondent man alive for some time. Ah, that's enough to cheer me up! I'd rather face years of another foreign war than what's at hand, but it's too late to pack the duffle and sign up now, isn't it, men?"

The four standing above him had corrected their postures and uniforms as much as possible and were now trying not to smile, though it wasn't common for the admiral to need encouragement.

"Admiral, Miss Smith is waiting outside," Nedrick reminded him.

"Quite naturally," he replied calmly, "the door's locked and she can't get in herself." The five of them slowly looked to the hallway as if this were an option, but he took a quick breath and exhaled it. "Admiral to the engine room, full ahead! Downs, let Smitty in. The rest of you, take your places. Remember, Major, suck it in! Stand behind something! Don't breathe! You're a highly ranked officer in these United States Armed Forces! If I can hold my water tonight, you can do the impossible, too!"

"Yes, sir." They looked all at each other, and grinned.

Major Downs strode across the burgundy-colored carpet while grossly protruding his chest. He corrected his hat and checked his buttons once as he turned the corner from the parlor into the foyer. He gripped the handle of the wide, oak door, but in looking beyond it, the teasing was forgotten and he had to ease to a wide grin.

A smiling Junie was standing on the patio with a white sweater draped over her arm, and a three-quarter length soft green evening dress complimenting her figure. She wore high heels, and he smelled a floral perfume. Some of her hair was brushed up into a barrette, the rest fell with a sheen to her shoulders, and the colors worked very well together. The neck and back of the dress were conservatively scooped, and her skin showed itself clear with a few faint freckles peeking from behind a necklace. The sleeves were to her elbows, very loose and fluid. She wore more cosmetics than last time, and she appeared confident and very welcome of a glamorous evening. She was a perfect match for the group awaiting her, yet what was always the most compelling about Junie was her happy and reassuring manner.

"Good evening, Miss Smith. I am pleased to welcome you back."

"Thank you, Major. You look very nice!" She smiled at him, impressed.

A palm aided the vain retraction of his stomach region, though it was more to cover than to correct now. "I must return the compliment, Miss. Please come in. May I take your wrap?"

"Thank you, sir, yes." She stepped in and passed him the sweater. As he turned from her, she again smoothed the imitation satin fabric over her legs and checked the strand of plastic pearls she wore. She felt she was entering the house for the first time, and its fine décor only helped her poise. The dress was the only one she owned, and while it was more than a few years old and second hand, the classic style fit her well and she liked the cut on her figure. She smiled when the major refaced her. "This must be your army uniform, sir?" she asked.

Major Downs came before her, redefining his profile to its best, yet now feeling it unnecessary. His nervousness was relieved, and he was looking forward to the evening. "Yes, Miss. I'm flattered you remember my branch. Thank you."

Junie smiled all the more. "I am the one who's flattered, Major! I don't get a chance to have nights like this very often, but it must be a bother to everyone else. It really is unnecessary, too. I wouldn't have changed a thing about last week. I had a wonderful time coming here and meeting all of you, no matter the circumstances. I thank *you*, sir."

His greeting was made warmer, and soon the tailoring

would be forgotten completely. "Thank you, Miss Smith. If you would come this way, the admiral and the others await you. It will be my pleasure to present you."

He extended his elbow, and Junie grasped it with a new smile. They went the short distance and turned to their right to stand in the wide entry of the large parlor.

She hadn't seen this room before, and her quick glance around before being announced, thrilled her. The plaster walls were a gentle off-white, the sculpted carpet elegant in itself, a granite fireplace showed a glowing blaze, and two large bay windows nestled in the far corner were bursting with colorful flowers selected by her escort that afternoon. She smiled at him in knowing this. The furnishings were beautiful reproduction antiques, and the high ceiling had a cornice trim that held long cords from which the many oil paintings portraying ships at sea and battle scenes were hung. Near them was a wet bar, made of a mahogany with a gorgeous grain.

"Admiral Crimmins and fellow officers, may I announce the arrival of Miss Smith."

They had taken positions by their favorite chairs, all but the admiral remaining on their polished shoes. They faced her sharply, and the admiral came spinning toward her while tooting the horn in rapid measure. Her aura had the same effect on him as it had on the major, and his tension instantly dissipated.

"Ensign Junie! My dear, you're a sight for sore eyes, indeed! This is a pure delight, isn't it men? This is marvelous." He stopped in front of her and she clasped his hands and gave him his kiss on the cheek. He loved the eyes that twinkled at him.

"Hello, Admiral. Thank you. If I look half as good as everyone else, I'm more than satisfied!" She smiled at him, and then around to the others. They nodded to her in turn.

He kissed the back of both hands to her merriment. "There's no need to put it to a vote, I'm sure! Tonight I shall call you Princess Ensign Junie! Come in, come in, and let's gather 'round. I have been counting the hours until this evening since last week! I almost started cooking the food myself, but Harvey beat me off with a stick, wisely enough. Come here, dear, and sit for a few minutes."

Before leaving the major, Junie smiled at him, and then let the admiral tug her by the hand to an open Queen Anne he saved for her. He put his wheelchair next to it and waited for her to sit down.

"If you don't mind, sir, I'd like to greet everyone again." She smiled as she stepped from him, starting to her left where the lieutenant was standing a half dozen steps from her. He straightened himself as she approached, and firmly clasped the hand she offered him. "Lieutenant Harvey, it is very nice to see you again."

"Thank you, Miss." He shook it after removing his hat. "We're very happy to have you back."

"I think the sour cream is going to remain in the refrigerator tonight, won't it, Lieutenant?" She giggled.

He smiled. "I certainly hope so, Miss. Thank you. I hope the menu meets with your approval."

"I have no doubt everything will be perfect just the way you've planned it. Thank you for this evening, sir. You're very becoming in your navy uniform. I'm very grateful for all the work you put into everything tonight. I'm very, very flattered by all of you."

"You're welcome, Miss. Thank you." His eyes shone into hers, and this remained after she squeezed his hand and smiled to him a last time before continuing on to the captain.

Nedrick's usual chair was at an angle where he could

observe the activity of the room and enjoy the fireplace. It was a casually large chair, overstuffed, and his cane leaned unused against the wide arm of the dark upholstery. A foot stool had been put to the side.

"Captain Nedrick, it's very nice to meet you again, too, sir," she said, taking his hand. "It's fortunate for me that you all represent so many different branches of the service. The uniforms are stunning. I thank you, Captain, for agreeing to do this for me tonight."

He looked down at her and grinned politely. The pale color of her dress brought out the green of her eyes and the reddish highlights of her hair, and he didn't welcome noticing such things this time. She had just vanquished two of her critics, and her honesty was further complicating his chores for the evening. He had talked himself hoarse in practicing his presentation, and without use of a single wile, in the space of fifteen minutes, using a handful of basic words, every hesitance but his was gone. He had witnessed Harvey wink at Downs for the impact she was having, and he felt alone in expecting the evening's outcome to be one of total failure. He wanted to frown, but the hand gripping his had the opposite effect. He would add his name to her list of friends with his own pen. He smiled politely.

"Thank you, Miss Smith, and it is our pleasure to do so for you. Please consider us at your disposal. Even if someone else needs lifesaving measures tonight."

They chuckled together. "Thank you, but I hope not! Speaking of that, sir, how is your recovery going concerning your hip? I understand you still face surgery."

He remained as welcome for this subject as the other, though it was unusual for him. "I have no complaints, Miss, and I thank you for your thoughtfulness."

Junie released his hand with a kind grin. "I'm very glad

for that, Captain. I'll think all good thoughts for you. Thank you again, sir."

"You're very welcome, Miss." As she moved on, he caught the glimpses of both Downs and Harvey. He gave their tickled expression a lightly scolding glance.

The last stop of Junie's nearly full circle was Colonel Harrison, and he was awaiting her with a beaming smile. She took the steps to him and held his outstretched hand in both of hers. She had wanted to greet each man to eliminate any remainder of shame from the week before, but Colonel Harrison she especially wanted to speak to as he had been the most distressed. "Colonel, it is so nice to see you again."

His smile couldn't broaden more. "Oh, Miss Smith, it's my pleasure! And may I thank you for returning, and the admiral for extending your invitation to include us? It is a great treat to see you again, truly."

She giggled at his enthusiasm and release from embarrassment. "Colonel, if we're near any of your artwork tonight, please tell me. I really do envy your ability. Admiral Crimmins tells me you were in charge of the whole house redecoration. If this beautiful room is any indication of your talent, I will be as awed as the admiral is."

His eyes grew larger, and he shook her hand with fervor. He was easily moved by any compliment to the only thing he had to love, and tightness formed in his throat. "Miss Smith, I would be only too happy to oblige you. Thank you for what you just said. Thank you, too, Admiral, for the compliment."

Admiral Crimmins sounded the horn with an exaggerated nod. "There's a fine man, Harrison! Ensign I find it beyond thanks that our glorious country saw fit to assign belts to our uniforms. If not, my men and I would have faces as red as flag stripes for having the pants charmed off us! Come and sit down, Princess Ensign Junie, and hold my hand for a little while. I'll fight to the last for the privilege, and I beg you the favor. Downs, how about our drinks now? Harvey? How about the vittles, son? Is everything on cruise control, or should the flames be stoked?"

When Junie sat in the Queen Anne, Harrison and Nedrick took their chairs as well. Down and Harvey remained standing, and she smiled as she obliged the admiral by taking the gentle hand he held out to her.

Lieutenant Harvey replaced his hat. "If you will excuse me, I'll go begin my final preparations for serving. It won't be more than fifteen minutes, sir."

"Excellent! Get to the chore, lad!" He tooted the horn.

"Yes, sir. Admiral. Officers. Miss." He touched his fingers to his hat in respect, but left with a smile shared only with Junie.

Major Downs stepped toward her to offer his services. "May I mix you a cocktail, Miss Smith?"

"By all means, Ensign, order tall!" the admiral invited. "I've never seen the man fail as a bartender. Every known concoction from Dover to Denver is child's play to him. He even has little umbrellas and sticks with plastic fruit on them down under that cabinet! Think of something wild to stump him, and we'll all belly up!"

She laughed, but would ask the major's advice. "I'm not much of a drinker, sir, and later I'll be driving myself home. If you could recommend something mild, that will do until the next time, please."

He nodded with a smile, knowing what would be proper. "We have a sweet white wine that may be to your liking, Miss. It's a smooth drink, and it won't counter anything the lieutenant is serving tonight."

Junie agreed. "I'll try that, please, sir. Thank you."

"You're welcome, Miss Smith. Admiral, your nightly scotch, sir?"

"Without delay, quite naturally, thank you, lad. Men, join us. We'll toast the lady."

"Gin and tonic, Major, thank you," Colonel Harrison said.

"My usual, Downs," the captain added.

"The major set to his task.

"Ensign, before the evening is through, you should have a tour of the various works done by Colonel Harrison. At another time, I'd like to show off the entire house to you. I know you've liked it from the beginning, and it's few and far chances between that it gets to sport itself.

"This is our humble parlor, as you can see. I collected these paintings from around the world, at different ports I've been stationed. Should the place burn down, I'll be here trying to pry them from their nails, to be sure. The older I get, the more pleasure they give me, just like good artwork should.

"And speaking of that, out back Harrison has his art studio. Rather impressive it is, too, and stocked with every pot of color known to man, and then some of his own mixing, of course. Rows and stacks of—what do you call those square things, Hezekiah?"

"Canvases, sir," he supplied happily.

"Yes, what a fine memory you have, Hezekiah, thank you. Rows and stacks and various canvases he has out there, ready to be a genius on, and he'll do it, too. You'll have to see it.

"Attached to it is Downs' greenhouse, or hothouse, whatever he wants to dub it. Every finger is green, as you know. You've never seen the gadgets he has in there to trim and plant and do all sorts of things with. Mother Nature always stands at attention when he goes out there! Good thing he wasn't a mad scientist, or he'd have blown up the world by now. Thank you, Major," he said as he and Junie were handed their beverages.

"For not being a mad scientist, or for the drinks, sir?" He smiled at Junie and they laughed together.

"They're one and the same at the moment, lad! Good wit there, too." The horn sounded as if a pat on the back.

"I thank you, too, Major," Junie added with a smile.

"You're welcome, Admiral. My pleasure, Miss Smith." He grinned at her and went on to serve the colonel and the captain.

Admiral Crimmins finished his verbal tour. "If you're a hiker, Smits, someday take a walk to the pond. Our property stops along its shores, and I've seen the drop of water on my land specs, but I've never found it in person. It's supposed to be stocked with a diversity of aristocratic fish, and nothing can be built directly on it. Can only use motor-less crafts there. Hopefully, it's a pretty little sight. Whatever prevented me from going down there I can't tell you, but someone will have to do it in order to make sure the street name is honest.

"In the meantime, we're all sitting here with a full glass in our hands, and I say bottoms up, everyone! To our newest friend, Miss Junie Bernice Smith!" He held up his tumbler.

"Here, here!" the colonel spoke out.

"To your health, Miss Smith," Captain Nedrick agreed.

"Wishing you happiness, Miss," Major Downs said with a nod, obediently imbibing on ice water.

Junie smiled with delight. "Thank you very much, and to the health and happiness of you all, too."

They had taken a few swallows when Lieutenant Harvey

appeared. "Admiral, may I invite you and everyone else to be seated, please?"

The horn sounded royally for the announcement and the perfect timing. The admiral called for everyone to bring their drinks, and he passed his to the colonel so he could lead Junie out of the room. He turned into the spacious hallway, and stopped before a closed double-doorway to their left. When all were gathered, he nodded and the lieutenant stepped in while opening the doors.

Junie had to gasp. The admiral beamed himself when seeing her reaction, and he allowed Harvey to escort her to her seat as he transferred himself from his wheelchair into the high-back at his normal place. There was a corsage beside her plate, and the lieutenant pinned it on her with her permission.

The dining room was thoroughly formal. Dark cherry wood paneling covered the walls, exquisite with detailed trim, and a light oak parquet floor set the shades to their best advantage. The table was a huge expanse of oak, it was a soft oval, and could set twelve without extensions. Two large silver and crystal candelabras decorated each end, and a matching chandelier hung from the center of the tin plated ceiling. The lighting was dimmed, and classical music played quietly in the background.

Admiral Crimmins was at the head of the table, Junie to his left, Colonel Harrison to her left, and Lieutenant Harvey would sit beyond him so to be in proximity to the door that swung into the kitchen. Captain Nedrick was at the admiral's right side, with Major Downs beyond him. When Junie was seated, Lieutenant Harvey pushed in her chair, the other men sat down, and Harvey took the wheelchair from the room and returned to serve the first course.

There was a duck and barley soup that night, followed

by a beautifully presented salad with his own dressing, and braided rolls and sweet butters served by the very hands that fashioned them. The main course was a fruited chicken—chosen because the admiral knew she liked the filets—with baby red potatoes, buttered fresh carrots, and, for the admiral, a pineapple cottage cheese, one of his favorites. It was a staple of every meal in some portion.

Each man soon became casual and attempted topping the other with stories of their active service years, and by the time the dessert of chocolate mousse with fresh raspberry and mint sauces was sent to digestion, the jackets that could be unbuttoned were, and Junie had her heels off under the table. An after-dinner brandy was passed by the major with small, individually wrapped parcels of hand-made chocolates. Laughter was so abundant their stomachs could ache from that alone. The admiral was a perfect host, and Lieutenant Harvey was very attentive to her needs during the meal. Major Downs saw to her iced tea as they ate, and the colonel and the captain warned the others to edit their tales, with the colonel being a charming side partner. The six became fonder of each other, every one pleased that their personalities fit together so easily.

"One more story has to come for Miss Smith, Admiral," the major said in helping his friend clear the last dish from the table. The constrictive jacket was removed altogether, to his sheer relief.

"And which is this, lad?" Admiral Crimmins was rubbing his own small abdominal area while resting his head back against the chair.

"The story of how you got your tooter, of course."

The others chuckled and agreed. "You should have started with that one, sir," the captain said, looking over to Junie and nodding. "That's as calm a story as any we've told tonight."

Junie laughed with anticipation. "Admiral, you must tell me! I thought there must be a reason behind it. I'll bet it's from your beloved naval days, correct?"

He nodded once, firmly. "Quite naturally, and I owe you a toot for such superb guessing. Your reward is that I'll tell you the honest version." He quieted, letting the room become more subdued. He leaned forward in his chair. The men around him chuckled for the unnecessary sobriety. "And it's a short one, so we won't take up the rest of the evening, though I've been known to stretch it out for great lengths of time, haven't I, men?"

"Without effort," Nedrick said with hearty agreement.

The admiral laughed. "Well, then let me begin for our dear Smits. I love this story myself, so if I ever forget it, it's time to roll me down to the mysterious pond and put an anchor around my feet and shove me in.

"I was a youth of seventeen when I signed up, Ensign. I knew since I was a toddler of two and saw my first cutter that naval service was in my blood. I lied about my age and raised a few eyebrows along the way, but being it was a time of war in the European theater, they weren't questioning much.

"I flew through basic. I loved it. I loved every bead of sweat, every strained muscle, every command and detail of it, though you had to complain, and bitterly, too, or you were considered a dolt. Would do it again today if they'd take me! It wasn't long until I was assigned to my first ship. A little thing, she was, held a crew of no more than fifty. Packed in like sardines, we were, but I knew almost all of the men, and those I didn't soon were like brothers to me. But I became the brunt of all their jokes on the first night out.

"I wish I could tell you there was a storm of magnificent

proportions, but the bay was as flat as God ever made it. I had a dream that night, and remembering dreams is so unusual for me that I believed it through and through. The ship had been hit fatally, and we were afire and going down flank speed. I ran from bunk to bunk, yelling, yanking, getting everyone up, and until finally—WHAM!—that dream was over! I had been hit so hard I didn't wake up for a full day.

"In the infirmary the nurses were bent over me and wondering if they should call for last rites. When I woke up, I could see only out of little slits, and my head was in such splitting pain I thought maybe I should just let myself go.

"Turns out I had been acting out that dream, of course. I single-handedly scared all the new crew members half to death, and caused a few to even panic and jump overboard! The midshipman on watch had no other way to stop me but to punch me square in the nose. I was hit so hard my proboscis was actually indented to the right side, and the little bone was reduced to near powder. My eyes ballooned and my sinuses filled with blood, three front teeth were loose, and it could have been nip and tuck there for a while, but I woke up and everyone began ignoring me as usual again. The commander so marveled at my courage and selflessness that I was promoted right there in my infirmary bed! But, best of all, the midshipman who did it felt so bad to nearly send me under that he gave me a horn, similar to what I have today, to make up for losing my 'honker' for a spell! Funniest thing that ever happened to me! They told me to have some surgery to fix the deviation that came of it, but I couldn't. Just couldn't. It was a good time, and I like the little crooked thing the way it is. It still works, and that's all that matters to me.

"And there you have it, Princess Ensign Junie, as simple

and truthful as it really happened. I dare say these men have never heard it told like that before!"

Junie laughed and even applauded him, and the others joined in. It was a good story to end the admitted exaggerations with, and they all calmed and took their last swallows, ending their dinner.

The admiral cleared his throat and glanced at Captain Nedrick. "Dear," he began, turning his attention back to their guest, "there is another conversation of great consequence that took place today, and I think it's high time we tackled it. Nedrick? Now's the time, my boy. Let's take the bull by the horns. No beating around the bush, cut right to the chase. What do you say, men? Let's get to the business at hand."

All eyes went to the captain who noticeably stiffened. "Sir...perhaps it would be best to...I'm wondering if...just what if..."

"Excellent idea, son!" the admiral shouted, and then turned to Junie. "The boy's a marvel, Smits, always a light bulb on over his head! Get to your gimpy feet, boy, and produce the supplies! Let's all make ourselves comfortable! Princess Ensign Junie, if you would bear with the boy for a few minutes, he'd like to explain something to you. He's speaking on my behalf because he has a way with legalities that I don't, but mainly because if you get mad, I want you to blame him! That way we could still be fast friends. After all, I'm an old man and should be forgiven for my lapses, but someone of his age is supposed to be more reliable and trustworthy.

"There we go, boy! The lady is completely prepared! In the end, I helped you quite a bit. Fire at will!"

The captain frowned heavily while raising himself from his formerly inviting chair. "'Fire at will', indeed," he muttered, gathering his cane to him. "If you will excuse me, the materials I need are just in the breakfront in the hallway. Sirs. Miss. I'll be less than a minute."

Junie simply looked from him to the admiral. The eldest officer cleared his throat loudly, then looked to her and smiled apprehensively, and glanced at his other men. Junie followed suit, a grin flickering over her face for the few widened eyes that avoided her. Colonel Harrison shifted in his seat, and seemed to creak as he did so.

Captain Nedrick returned in the time stated. He had a number of manila folders in his hands, and he stepped behind Admiral Crimmins to place one before him, then Junie, Harrison, Harvey, then he retraced his walk to hand one to Downs and himself. "Please don't open them until I'm ready, if you would. Thank you." Everyone looked down at the covers and saw their names printed on a gummed label affixed on the tab and in the center of the cream-colored heavy paper.

He took a deep breath, coughed, pulled up his chair, and took another breath. He closed his eyes for a moment, then spread his palms over his folder and appeared to give his manicure an examination. He cleared his throat and forced himself to begin.

"Miss Smith, it is a popular habit of the admiral not to mince words, and so, in honoring him, and because I am speaking for him, I will follow his example. Before you is a proposal of an agreement. It is an unorthodox document in the fact that it is of our making, though it is taken from a legal transcript used by lawyers and their clients to lawfully bind their understandings, and the admiral and I, over a great deal of time, have constructed these pages with care, thought, generosity, and even compassion, I hope. It was guided by me, with the limited knowledge of my self-taught hobby, but molded by him, with the heart that he has.

"As you might surmise, and as we plainly see justified, the admiral has become quite fond of you. One of the purposes of this dinner tonight was to prove why, and it's as clear as ever that Admiral Crimmins is a man of extraordinary taste, judgment, and good fortune. Without doubt, this document was created with the hopes of being offered to you, and it is only fitting that tonight you and it should meet."

He stopped, glanced around him for the reactions thus far, and felt his speech going well until catching the bemused expression on Major Downs' face. He gave the man to his right a frown. To his relief, the admiral seemed very pleased, and then he looked at Junie.

She smiled at him. She was being supportive. His brow was beaded with sweat, and for the first time that evening, his attractive uniform and studiousness likened to be someone else's second skin. Perhaps because of the order in which she had met him, he was her favorite of the group after the admiral, and she didn't want him upset. She believed all the men sincere, and she felt no harm would come to her in their presence. She wanted him to relax as he had been just a few minutes before when they had been enjoying the gaiety of their dinner.

Her encouragement was gladly accepted. Captain Nedrick straightened in his chair and took the folder in his hands. "Please open the cover. I'll read it aloud, Miss Smith, and that should explain what this is. I only ask the great favor of a full reading, with any questions coming after I'm done. Are you ready, Admiral?"

"Yes, boy! Good luck to us!" He smiled profusely, reaching to pat Junie's hand. He thumped on the table with his other. "I miss that honker of mine! Pretend, Ensign! This would be the greatest toot of all!"

She smiled. "All right, sir. I'll listen as you wish, Captain. Please go ahead."

There was a title page, but not a title. He simply started with:

"*'For all purposes of this contract, Miss Junie Bernice Smith shall be known as the Female Subject (abbreviated as FS), and Admiral Robert Adam Crimmins, United States Navy (R), shall be known as the Male Subject (abbreviated as MS).'*

"Miss Smith, in the event this becomes formal, I must ask if your given name is June or Junie?"

"June, sir," she supplied cordially.

"Thank you." He took a metallic pen he had clipped to his breast pocket, unscrewed the cap, and put a slash over the small I in her first name. "If we're all comfortable, let's turn the page and begin the reading."

"Um, Captain, may I ask a question before you begin, please?" she spoke after a quick glance around her. As there seemed to be a shared sense of tension, this made her question feel urgent. "I'm very sorry, and I promise I won't interrupt you again, but may I please ask something?"

He appeared slightly surprised, but consented. "Yes, Miss Smith?"

Junie grinned. "This 'contract' is supposed to be between Admiral Crimmins and myself, correct?"

"Yes, it is."

"Well, it looks like everyone but me knows what it's about. Can I at least ask what the general idea of this is?"

She was focused on him, and consequently saw him shift his posture in his chair. The Admiral waited, Colonel Harrison squirmed noisily in his seat once more, and Lieutenant Harvey looked at his lap in an attempt not to smile. Major Downs sat forward, leaned his head onto a palm, and gazed at her, only making the effort not to burst out laughing.

Captain Nedrick took a deep breath, held it, and then said in a blurting: "Ah... No."

"Gesundheit!" the Major said. More to his amusement, he got a horrible grimace from the captain.

She giggled. "No?" She looked to Admiral Crimmins.

He only shrugged. "He's handling this, my dear!" He thumped the table once more. "Remember, blame him!" The captain wanted to tsk at the shirking.

Her glance to the colonel revealed him cringing in supposed pain, the lieutenant had his smiling lips clamped between his teeth, and the major chortled once and tried to cover his mild hysteria by rubbing his forehead.

"May we please proceed, Miss Smith?" Nedrick asked, perturbed at everyone around him.

Junie only sighed and grinned. "Of course, sir. I'm sorry. Please go right ahead." They both looked at Major Downs, Nedrick with a scowl, and Junie with a pursed grin of gratitude.

The captain began his four page reciting:

"'*Section One: Fertility. Before either of the identified parties put their legal signatures to this contact, medical testing of the following specifications must be undertaken:*

"*1. The FS must be found capable of attempting to conceive, conceiving, and safely bearing and bringing to full gestational term one (1) child, heretofore known as the heir, for the MS listed.*

"*2. The MS must be found capable of producing a sufficient amount of spermatozoa to make the conception of the heir highly probable. In addition, these spermatozoa must be examined to ensure, as much as medically possible, the good health of the heir. Due to the recognized advanced age of the MS, this fertility testing will be done every three (3) months, and upon the request of the*

FS. If, at any time, the MS's fertility is found to be decreased to the point of ineffectiveness, the FS's responsibility to him is terminated, though she shall still be compensated as stated in Section Six, Number 3 (three).

"3. In the event the FS is found to be incapable of safely continuing with this contract, all reasonable efforts will be made to immediately terminate this agreement, with any resolution and/or compensation to be decided upon by both parties or an arbitrator, whichever is believed to be the most unbiased."

The captain had finished with the first section, and he made an instant scan of Junie. Her face was decidedly lowered, her eyes wide and eyebrows high, and when she looked at him with this shocked expression, his composure began to waiver. In this brief silence, he suddenly noticed the music had changed from Beethoven's "Pathetique" to his Symphony Number Five. The movement of Junie's eyes said she recognized it also, and he shot a panicked look to Harvey that pleaded for the soundtrack to be taken off more expeditiously than immediately. The lieutenant stood and silently did so, his shoulders shaking with suppressed laughter. Captain Nedrick went on as quietly as possible.

"Section Two: The Goal. The FS is hereby agreeing to attempt to conceive, bear, and give birth to an heir by the MS. Unless stated here, or in an amendment of later attachment, this heir is of every preference to be of the male gender, and so the FS shall make all medically recognized preparations to increase the probability of this outcome.

"Section Three: Conception. Conception of the heir will be attempted in either of the following manners:

1. Artificial insemination to be conducted in a doctor's office by a recognized professional; or

2. Sexual intercourse, henceforth known as the Business Transaction (abbreviated as BT). The BT shall be conducted as exactly that, with the FS having full discretion for its occurrence. The BT's will continue in an orderly fashion until an authenticated pregnancy is achieved. These BT's will be made as often as the MS is comfortable with; however, the FS shall determine the setting and method in which the BT is completed. If, at any time, any part of the BT is misconstrued by the MS, the FS has every right to terminate this agreement without explanation. Post Note to this section: In the event of recognized illness, injury, or other feminine concerns, the FS has the right to temporarily decline the BT with the MS.'"

Junie couldn't help but snort out a nervous laugh. Major Downs and Lieutenant Harvey tried not to join her, and the others looked to her with worry. "I'm sorry," she whispered to the captain, who tried to disguise his panic by fawning insult. "It's the letters. FS, MS, BT… I'm sorry, sir. Please go on." Blushing, she looked back to the papers she was holding.

His eyebrow was raised. "We're half done, Miss Smith?"

She nodded, gripping the pages more firmly. "Certainly, Captain. Please."

He gave her a discontented look before going back to his task.

"'Section Four: Lifestyle During This Contract.

1. The FS shall reside legally and full-time at the address of the MS during the lifetime of this contract.

2. The FS shall be given a private suite of rooms which shall include a bedroom, a full bathroom, and a spare room suitable for an office or parlor, to be decorated in the style of her preference. All expenses for said redecoration will be incurred by the MS.

3. The FS shall live in a clean, healthy, and respectable manner, and make every possible effort to ensure a safe and healthy gestation and birth.

4. The FS shall live in the same accordance during lactation, if this preferred option is chosen by the FS.

5. The FS shall make every reasonable effort to live harmoniously with the MS and all other occupants of his household.

6. The FS has the right to socialize with her other acquaintances of good moral standing during the day, but sexual intercourse is strictly forbidden.

7. The FS shall not show any preference or displeasure to the MS, or any other occupant of his household. She shall treat all the occupants with equality.

8. The MS, or any other occupant of his household, may not compete for the attention or affection of the FS.

9. No part of this contract is to be construed or acted upon as a romantic involvement, and feelings of emotional attachment are not allowed.

"'Section Five: Determination of Parentage.

"'1. At the medically predetermined date during gestation, the FS shall submit to having the necessary test(s) performed which will state the gender, physical condition, and parental identification of the heir. Once this identification has been made, the MS has the exclusive right to decide the fate of the gestation. Any disagreement by the FS to this decision shall sever the MS's responsibility to the FS and the heir.

"'2. The MS has the right to correct, advise or otherwise guide the lifestyle of the FS during the tenure of the gestation as to her health, the health of his heir, and the mental state of the FS.

3. The MS has the exclusive right to name his heir.

"'Section Six: Post-Delivery and Compensation. 1. The FS shall, if possible and desirable to her, nurse the heir for at least three (3) months after his birth.

2. At the end of these same three (3) months, the FS may legally, in writing, relinquish all or part of her parental rights of the heir, and her responsibilities will dissolve.

3. The FS shall be paid the sums of: Five thousand dollars ($5,000) by the MS the day of the initial insemination or BT takes place; Five thousand dollars ($5,000) upon authenticated conception and paternal identification of the heir; and Twenty thousand dollars ($20,000) for the live birth of the heir and the three months care following the live birth, for a total of thirty thousand dollars ($30,000) to be paid in any manner chosen by the FS.

4. All medical expenses for the FS and the heir are the responsibility of the MS.

"<u>Section Seven: Contract Tenure.</u> The contract shall be in effect from the moment the identified parties have signed until the moment all said parties have deemed the goal fulfilled to its greatest potential. In this event, every copy of this contract shall be produced and jointly destroyed by means of incineration.'"

Captain Nedrick was finished. Junie's face remained bowed over the pages, and she heard him rest back in his chair with such relief, the movement knocked his cane from the arm. It clattered on the parquet floor, unrescued. Out of the corner of her eye, she could see him close his folder and fan his entire upper body with it. He loosened his collar and exhaled.

She knew the others must be waiting for her, but she had to take her time. When she did raise her head, she looked only to the admiral. The captain's fanning stopped. She took a slow, deep breath, preparing them both, and she made her expression warm, kind, and her voice tender when she addressed him. Any mirth had left the room far before the dropping of Nedrick's cane.

Junie extended her hand over the table, and the admiral, a sad glint coming into his eyes, took her hand with the both of his. The speech that came from her was formed with her genuine care for him. She had been able to think during the reading as her response had been nearly instantaneous.

"Sir, I've heard if a gentleman was going to propose a serious commitment to a lady he deeply cared for, he'd wear his best clothes, wine her and dine her, give her flowers and candy, and put his very best foot forward. I know, Admiral Crimmins, this is what you did for me tonight. You even asked your good friends for help, and they were wonderful to add to it for us.

"I'm certain, as time goes by, that I'll be very, very flattered and moved by this, sir. I know it's a great, great compliment for a man such as you to ask someone to give him a child, even by surrogacy, which I guess this is. But...I really don't need time to think about it.

"Sir, you are seventy years old. I don't mean to hurt you, I really don't, but I don't know if a man your age should become a father. This may be judgmental and I deplore that in anyone, but you've had a landmark birthday, and you might be taking stock of your life. It must be very sad that the crews are gone, there are no more ships to command, and you're alone when you go to bed at night. You've surrounded yourself with other men in the same situation, but it's not enough, is it?

"You alone know why you missed out on having a family. I'm not asking, and I don't need to know. I'm sorry to say I think the time has passed for this, sir. I'm sure you must have always thought of your crew first because that's the kind of man you are, and now you must think of this child. It's such a monumental job, and it goes on for such a long time...I've only babysat myself, but raising a responsible, well-adjusted person takes a lifetime of devotion and sacrifices. It's never something to do just for your own fulfillment.

"Please don't be hurt. I don't want that. I am very fond of

you as a friend, Admiral Crimmins, and I want to always be able to count on that. You can count on it from me, I promise you. All of you can. I am very fond of everyone in this room."

Junie stood, caressed his cheek, and she waved to the others so they wouldn't rise with her. Colonel Harrison moved only to take the heavy chair from her way. Her grin to them was tinged with pain for all of them, including herself.

"I've probably ruined the evening for all of you, so I should go. It's very late for me, anyway. I have to be at work at six a.m. I'll never forget tonight, and I thank you, Admiral, and everyone for what you did. Lieutenant Harvey, the meal was the best I've ever had. Major Downs, thank you for serving me so well. Colonel Harrison, you are a lovely dining partner. Captain Nedrick, your document and reading was very good. And Admiral..." she stepped to give him a long kiss on his cheek, "I really do care a great deal about you. Thank you for one of the best nights of my life. Good night, sweetheart. Please stay here. I'll see myself out, thank you."

He squeezed her hand, looking away. "Thank you, my dear. Drive safely. Please come back soon," he answered quietly.

She walked from her place, and even Major Downs thought his heart was lowering in his chest. They nodded to her, and Captain Nedrick reached for his cane.

"Please, Miss Smith, if I may walk you out?"

"It's not necessary, Captain. Thank you." She paused at the double doors of the exit to answer him.

"I'll admit it's for my sake, please, Miss. May I?" He went to his feet once more.

Junie reluctantly agreed, steadying her composure. She

didn't know why, but she felt like weeping. She took another long inhalation, and waited, not looking toward him. He opened the door and let her out, and she stepped away, not wanting to look back. She went to the foyer and knew where to find her sweater. "I don't know if you wanted to speak any more, Captain. I don't know if there's anything more to say, but I need to go outside, please. I know the fountain is lit, and I'd like to see it."

Nedrick took a deep, quiet breath himself. His voice was gentle and considerate. "Of course. Please go where you wish, Miss Smith." He held open the door for her, and they stepped to the edge of the brick patio. The fountain was not disappointing, and the crickets added their song. The stars glistened in the cool blackness. "Thank you, Miss Smith," he began.

She sighed, couldn't raise her glance to him, but formed a small grin. "For what, sir?"

The captain put his cane in front of him and leaned on it with both hands. "I pictured you running from the house, screaming for the police, and the rest of us feeling like first class heels. I tried and failed to write a speech for the authorities who would undoubtedly come bashing in our door."

Junie laughed, and the sound of it in the night made him look at her and warm to a half-smile. "Then I'm glad that didn't happen!"

"No one is more grateful than me."

She calmed and patted his shoulder. "I really don't want him hurt, Captain. I would feel very badly if that were the case. I know the rest of you will try to cheer him up, and I want you to tell him that I still would enjoy seeing him. To tell you the truth, I thought what all that was going to be about was some kind of protection for him in case I had other ambitions, you know? I know what people must think when a person of my background and means befriends someone like him. I wanted to talk about it myself tonight, but I didn't know how to bring it up.

"I know you were very nervous about that in there, Captain. You are a wonderful, true friend to do what you did. The admiral and the others are lucky to know you, sir. I feel you deserve great credit, Captain Nedrick."

He only shook his head. "I didn't do that well, Miss Smith."

"Yes, you did!" Junie laughed again. "It wasn't your delivery at all. In fact, I might have run screaming if you'd been anything less! I don't like cold fish or red tape, and I don't think you're a stuffed shirt at all. You're standing here now, caring about what I feel, aren't you?" She tilted her head to gaze at him with a grin, and when his firmer expression relaxed, she smiled.

She continued: "No, you didn't fail, sir. I was certainly surprised at first, but you did very well. It was all very well written, and very thoughtful, too, I think. If the law is your hobby, perhaps now that you're retired, you should go to school for it."

The captain watched the water play and exhaled. "It came from a great deal of discussion between all of us, no more, Miss Smith. Perhaps that's why he wanted everyone there, besides safety in numbers! It's something we've all wanted to do at one time or another. We completely understand him. It's egotistical, perhaps, but I'm afraid we can afford to be. That doesn't make it right, I'm aware, but we're honest about it, anyway, and we do appreciate all the variables. It's brought on by us knowing others who have families and take a great deal of pride in them. You must have seen classmates or friends of yours marry and have children, so you know what it feels like."

Junie sighed, grinned, and looked at him. "I do, sir. Those are my babysitting experiences."

"Add a few decades and worrying about dying alone, and there you have it for us 'old coots', as the Admiral calls us." He chuckled.

She did, too, and looked up at him. "Thank you for coming out here, Captain. You explained more to me here than in there. Good night, sir." She gave him a kiss on the cheek, and turned for her car.

"Good night, Miss Smith. Thank you again. I hope we see you very soon."

Junie smiled at him before getting into her automobile. "Take care, Captain! Say goodbye for me to the others, and give the admiral my love."

Nedrick nodded, and she engaged the engine. She waved, and he returned the parting as she pulled out of the gate.

Inside, he opened the closet door and pushed the button to close the gates. He had opened them for her, and he had dreaded the chore. Now he dreaded closing her out.

The captain sighed and limped slowly to the dining room. Like the front parlor he had just passed, the room was empty and dark. Even the tablecloth was gone. The folders were piled at his place. He left them there.

Admiral Crimmins' suite was across from the dining room. He went to the door and knocked. There was no answer, and upon opening it, he found the interior completely black. He knew the admiral slept with a light on, so he hadn't entered the room as yet. He closed the weighted, carved piece of wood.

He went through the breakfast room and into the kitchen. It was dark in here also, but he could see the French doors opened and the admiral in his wheelchair under the jamb looking outside. He had turned on the lights to the gazebo. The lights were tiny white bulbs, resembling many strings of holiday lights, and they outlined the large, romantic structure beautifully. The admiral was beholding it.

"Sir?" Nedrick asked gently.

"I sent the others on, son. Don't bother with me. I'm going to sit here for a spell, that's all. Nothing to worry about, boy, if you were."

The captain came beside him and looked out into the garden and lawn beyond it. The moon wasn't full, but it lit that side of the house and bathed the grounds with a peace that was envied from the interior.

"Thank you for what you did tonight. It was top notch. Nary a fault throughout. I was very proud of you."

He flushed, not agreeing with the critique, but he wouldn't argue. "I'm sorry it didn't turn out the way you wanted, sir. I'm very sorry."

"No need to be! We'd want an upstanding young lady to do it, and yet an upstanding young lady wouldn't consider it. Son, I think you can deep six the contract. It really is a silly, selfish thing to do, isn't it? She was totally right. Totally.

"I had two serious chances. Long ago, years apart, two wonderful gals, and I passed all of it up. I was rising in the ranks, and I was ambitious. As the old saying goes, if I knew then what I know now! But that's neither here nor there. Was she upset? Will she ever come back? Have I insulted her beyond repair?"

Nedrick was confident in his nodding. "She wanted me to give you her love, and she meant it. She wants to see you again, she told me so herself. She does care about you,

Admiral. After tonight, there can't be a one of us that doesn't think so."

"Ah...!" The admiral closed his eyes with relief, and heartache. "Her friendship is a reward in itself. I'll take it, yes, indeed, I shall! We'll have to order from the Uncle very soon and request her excellent delivery. Yes, we'll have to do that very soon..." His voice trailed, and the younger man turned away to give him privacy. A prized dream of his had been put aside, and he understood how that felt.

"Can I do anything for you, sir?" he asked with care, putting his hand on his shoulder.

"No, thank you. The sun comes up on this side of the house. I've never seen it. I'm an early riser, but I've always busied myself at that time of the morning. I think perhaps I shall not miss it today. Get yourself some rest, Rodgers. All will be well with the sunlight. Carry on, my friend. Carry on." He patted his hand, and this dismissed him.

"Good night, Admiral." With a last glance, he left the elder gentleman.

The other officers had their own suites on the upper floors. Downs and Harvey were on the third floor, and he and Harrison had rooms on the second floor. Also on the second floor was the guest suite, and if Junie had decided to sign the contract, the door at the head of the stairway would have become hers.

The guest quarters were the least spacious, but they spanned the entire length of the house. It had a full bathroom in the front, with an east-facing bedroom, and the cozy parlor ran over the kitchen. To make up for the long but narrow line, Harrison had designed a small balcony, much on a European influence, with doors that opened before it.

In the time Captain Nedrick had lived in the house, he

had seen the door opened only by the cleaning service. He knew the balcony had a fine view of the back grounds and gazebo, and he felt it a loss that Junie wouldn't be occupying it.

He rounded the hallway on the second floor, passed Harrison's door, and went to his own. It opened into his office, and he remembered the pile of contracts on the dining room table. The admiral wanted them thrown away. He would go down early in the morning to retrieve them, and relegate the files to unseen storage.

For now, he went to his bedroom and didn't turn on the lights, hoping the scant glow from the moon would warm the emptiness.

Section Four: Junie's Version

[END JUNE]

Over a week later, Admiral Crimmins placed their usual order from Uncle Tony's. He requested it be brought by Junie, but the hostess informed him Junie was no longer the delivery person, and would not be allowed to leave her position. The admiral shouted at her, canceled the order, and retreated to his quarters for the rest of the evening. Lieutenant Harvey brought him a dish of cottage cheese with pineapple, even putting a maraschino cherry on top, but in the morning he discovered it untouched. The household lost the little progress it had made in the last few days.

Ten days after that, the intercommunication system box on the outside of the gate was used to buzz the home. Major Downs was walking from the kitchen to the parlor, and happened upon the noise. He went to the front door and pressed the speaker button. "Yes?"

"I have a delivery from Uncle Tony's restaurant, sir! I'd like to personally make up for what happened over a week ago, if I could. What wonderful officer am I speaking to, please?"

He could clearly see the brown car with the new white wall tires awaiting entrance, and the tone and joy of the voice was also recognized nearly immediately. He was smiling broadly. "You happen to be speaking to the wonderful Major Alan Downs, Miss Smith! Permission granted to come aboard, as the admiral would say!" He nearly jumped in place as he took his hand from the speaker and sent the gates into motion. He even pressed the button more than once with hopes it would encourage it to work more rapidly. "Saints preserve us!" he whispered happily.

He jogged to the front parlor, wanting to throw the sandwich he had just made for himself against the wall. It was seven p.m., and all but Colonel Harrison were gathered to eat and play their usual games of cards. The admiral was looking over a foreign newspaper, and he, Harvey, and Nedrick had been playing their first game of Knights. Harrison would be in his art studio for another hour. Downs nearly jumped into the wide entryway of the room. "Put down those cards, boys! We're having pizza in a few seconds!" he called, startling them all.

Harvey frowned. "What? I'm broiling scrod tonight. And you shouldn't be eating now, Downs, you'll spoil it. What happened to your diet, soldier?" He grinned at his friend.

The major only brightened his smile, turning to the admiral. "Damn the sandwich, damn the fish, and damn the diet! Something far better is on the way! Sir, would you like to greet the lady bringing you a garlic special?"

Cards and jaws did drop, and Admiral Crimmins didn't need a second to gasp and toss the paper to the floor. Through one of the bay windows, he could see the brown car coming to a halt and its driver getting out with a smile to get the boxes from the back seat. "Princess Ensign Junie!" he shouted, and blew the horn as often as he could while making his way to the foyer.

Major Downs went to his aid. He pulled open the front door, and Junie was nearly there, carrying six boxes of pizzas in her arms.

"Permission requested to enter and serve, sir! More vittles for the steadfast crew! Open the windows, Major

Downs, because I have an extra special garlic special in here!" She laughed as both men held out their arms. The major got the boxes and the admiral got his kiss.

"My dear! This is the best surprise I've had in absolute years!" The captain and the lieutenant were behind him now, and Harvey had used the intercom to summon the colonel.

"Thank you, Major. Hello, Captain. Hello, Lieutenant," she said to the faces smiling at her.

"Hello, Miss Smith!" came as one.

Junie now addressed the admiral. She was delighted to see him. "It's a nice evening, sir, and I've been promised a tour of the house, in and out. I hope this is a good time for you all. If not, I can just leave the pizzas. I should have called first, but I wanted to surprise you. Can we go out to the gazebo again, or we could eat in, if you'd rather?" She was holding both of his hands. Dressed in khaki slacks and a printed shirt tucked into the waist, she was casual and relaxed, as happy to see them as they were to see her.

"This is your night off, dear? And you want to spend it with a bunch of old coots?" the admiral asked her.

She laughed. "Yes, it is, sir, and I couldn't think of a better bunch of old coots to hang out with! If you're not doing anything, I'm bribing you by bringing dinner."

He dropped a hand only to use the horn. The sound rang over the driveway. "I know I can speak for the whole blasted mess of us and say no bribery needed, Ensign! Men! Prepare the gazebo! Cancel the President! Downs, shoo off the bees! Harvey, get out the chairs! Nedrick, waddle around doing something useful, and someone buzz that plain cheese pizza of a painter, Harrison!"

"That mission is already accomplished, sir," the major said as he departed with the boxes.

"Good man!" The others left to fulfill their duties, and the admiral took advantage of their time alone. He kissed her hands. "Ensign, I feared I wouldn't see you again. It has dampened my countenance considerably. I haven't been myself. Just this morning as I was shaving my dour expression, I said 'Who are you, man shaving with a dour expression?'" His smile was sweetly sad.

Junie shook her head with a warm grin. "I did let too much time pass, sir. I'm sorry. Please don't ever worry about that again."

"I know what I did to you. We'll put the unpleasantness behind us, shall we? Yes, we shall! You have made me very, very happy, dear. I've been moping around for what feels like an eternity. It's the darnedest business, being sad! I have good men around me and they mean well, but they are the clumsiest oxen when trying to do something emotional! 'Admiral, how about this?' 'Admiral, why don't we do that?' Under foot every moment! I've had more cottage cheese and sour cream brought to me than I've eaten in my entire life! I went from being sad to being mad all in the same minute! They're lucky it's a horn on this chair and not a pistol, is all I can say. They were even making the bed for me, and I haven't missed making my own bunk in sixty-eight years."

Junie laughed and squeezed his hands. "I hope they did a good job."

He frowned, shaking his head. "I haven't bounced any quarters in a week, Ensign. It's a darned shame. Bad for my reputation, quite naturally."

"Quite naturally! Well, you'll have to do it tomorrow, because if the windows aren't opened…!"

The Admiral laughed and began leading them to the kitchen. They were met there by the colonel, who was running in from his studio.

"Miss Smith! How good to see you!" His eyes were bright, and he huffed his breath for so quickly putting away his supplies and trotting there.

Junie laughed and went to him. He had a smudge of red on his chin, and she took the cloth sticking out of his shirt pocket and augmented its purpose. "Hello, Colonel. After dinner I'd like to start my grand tour with your paintings, if we could, sir?"

"Oh, most certainly! My pleasure!" He nearly clapped, and she kissed his cheek for his mood and greeting.

Five chairs and the wheelchair were set around the gazebo. As each person wanted food, they would take it from the boxes piled on the portable card table Lieutenant Harvey set up in the center. Junie had her iced tea, and the others had beer or ice water. All had great fun, and it was the most casual dinner the officers had shared since basic training.

"Major Downs, you look like you've lost weight, sir," Junie commented during the meal.

He played a frown. "I'm under strict orders to lock up my wheelbarrow and not enjoy sour cream any more, Miss Smith. What I am is sore and deprived!" They laughed. The conversation and mirth continued for another ninety minutes.

All helped clean up the boxes, and the crusts were thrown over the sides of the structure. The gazebo was framed not only by the major's prize-winning roses, but by a moat he had treated as a water garden. Lily pads and other aquatic flora bloomed there, and beneath the glassy surface swam a dozen colorful koi fish. The koi devoured the breadstuffs with an eager fight, and Junie laughed at seeing them. "Shark invested waters!" Admiral Crimmins warned her, smiling at her with delight.

Cans and glasses were piled on a tray on the senior officer's lap, and he said goodbye to her as Harrison, Downs, and Harvey took her for a walk around the outside of the property. She saw the art studio where the colonel was in the process of painting the very gazebo they had dined in. She was genuinely awed by his degree of ability, and he promised to present the finished work to her. The major's greenhouse was adjacent it, and he showed her his seedlings, grafting work, and other projects, plus his certificate on the registration of his namesake rose.

They pointed out the path that would take her to the pond, and she promised to venture it sometime soon if they wanted to go. Harvey offered a picnic, and they agreed to make a date. Back in the house, the admiral showed her the only rooms she hadn't seen of the downstairs, and that was his personal quarters. The six suites in the house consisted of a spacious bedroom, a full bath, and an office or parlor, as the contract had described.

The admiral's office was filled from floor to high ceiling with all sorts of pictures from his naval career: awards, commendations, books, and models. Hundreds of framed photographs covered nearly every inch of the room. Even at a quick glance, Junie recognized many political figures. His large bed had a replica of a ship's wheel at the headboard, and Colonel Harrison had seen to give the admiral a row of salvaged port holes above it. It was an impressive sight, and he was proud to show it to her.

Again he let her go as the others took her to the upper levels. On the second floor, Captain Nedrick's office seemed fit for any business with rows of legal books lining one wall, and miscellaneous items of office equipment taking another. Off of the office was his bedroom and bath, and they were also decorated by him with a masculine hand, darker colors, and marine memorabilia. His rooms faced the north side of the property, and appeared to be the most spacious of the house. It was impeccably clean, and to move something out of place would have caused the suite considerable discomfort, it seemed.

Colonel Harrison's rooms had a southern exposure, though he stated he enjoyed the view overlooking the driveway the most. The colors were almost a glaring contrast to the captain's: lighter in hues and many mixes, and was filled with whimsical wicker items and custom painted antiques. He didn't want an office, so he turned his spare room into his own library, and he showed her a few volumes of classic novels, some signed by their famous authors.

They returned to the stairs, not showing her the guest quarters in the event it remind her of her refusal, and Downs and Harvey showed her their rooms.

On the topmost floor there were ample storage rooms and two complete suites, one on each side of the house. The major was an admitted "collector of nothing in particular", as he explained before opening the door. He showed her many of his favorite items, of which were racing cars he had built from elaborate kits, sports team pennants and autographed pictures, and smaller versions of the flags from countries he had been stationed in. He had glass sculptures, a collection of Persian carpets, and embroidered pictures. Harvey joked that this side of the floor would soon cave in, and they laughed. It was very full, but there was so much to look at, boredom would not have been a problem for weeks of confinement.

Lieutenant Harvey's suite was again a contrast, and this time in starkness. His taste was for Shaker furniture and its appeal: simple, sparse, utilitarian, and clean. The only pictures he had on the walls were one Harrison had painted for him of a still life, and an enlarged photograph taken on the dock in front of his ship after his retirement party. In contrast to the others, there was very little that told he had spent his adult life in the service. There were 27 pegs along one long wall for hanging clothes should he adopt the plain lifestyle.

"The house is just beautiful, sir," Junie said upon returning to the admiral and captain, who waited for her in the parlor. They had set a fire, and she went over to the two bay windows. The flowers were gone from the weeks before, but she could see out, and she liked the fountain very much.

The rest of the floor in the room was carpeted, but here by the windows, under her feet, the marble tile of the foyer was used. She pictured a full Christmas tree there, and she thought perhaps its designer had this in mind when putting the two huge windows in this location. She wondered if men without families did such things. She smiled and turned back to them.

"If you'll excuse me, I have something I want to get from my car. Please stay here. I'll be right back, Admiral. Officers." Junie jogged out of the room and went out the front door.

They looked from one to the other, not knowing what she had in mind. She had refused reimbursement for the pizzas, and though they had foregone any desserts Lieutenant Harvey offered, they thought perhaps she had brought another treat.

She returned quickly, but with a single manila folder in her hand. She smiled. "Would you like me to sit here again, sir?"

They had taken their usual seats, and the admiral had picked up the paper and put himself next to the same Queen Anne he had saved for her before. "Quite naturally, dear!"

he said, adding a toot on the horn for her.

"I'd hold your hand, but I'm going to need mine for a minute or two." Junie smiled at him, and then looked at the faces watching her. In particular, she glanced at Captain Nedrick. She thought he may be able to guess since she had chosen his style. His eyes were narrowed with curiosity, and she believed he was forming ideas. As she spoke, she glanced from one interested expression to another.

"I haven't been able to think about much else but all of you since I was here last. I've come to the conclusion that I was mistaken about a few things, and I want to correct that and apologize tonight. I'm afraid I can't pass around copies like Captain Nedrick did because this is handwritten, but if things go well tonight, maybe he wouldn't mind getting copies made.

"I'm going to be a little different than the captain, though, and explain what this is all about. I've done a great deal of soul searching. For me, this means bringing up my past. It has always haunted me to some degree, but in this it came in very handy.

"I know firsthand that being young doesn't mean you'll be a good parent. I was abandoned at a hospital not too far from here on June first, twenty-five years ago. The nurses gave me the name of June because of it, and the state gave me Smith because 'Doe' had already been used a lot that year. They put June first as my birthday on the certificate they had to make for me. I don't know anything at all about my parents except that the guard on duty said my mother was very young, and when she did what she had to do, she jumped into a car driven by a young man. I've imagined all these years they were classmates who got in over their heads, but maybe that's romanticizing it too much.

"I went from one foster home to another. Because my

supposed parents had been seen, the state wanted to see if they would come forward at some point and reclaim me. They never did, but my status was never changed. I couldn't be adopted. The families I lived with were used to having children go in and out of their lives, and though most of them were good, I never got attached to any of them. I picked my middle name of Bernice, and just started using it one day. She was my second grade teacher, and the first person I ever remember embracing me. It's probably not legal, but from that moment that's what I called myself. It stuck the same as the other names and birthday I was given.

"It wasn't easy growing up that way, but when I got to my adult years, I decided either I survived it and made the best of everything, or I ruined the rest of my life by being angry. I only had myself, so I didn't want to wake up some day and realize I had blown it. I'm a strong person, and I'm proud that I can work very hard. I hope I have a talent in here somewhere, and I'm waiting to find it, or have it find me."

Junie paused, gazing at the admiral, and seeing him nod with support for her. His expression was thoughtful.

Feeling confident, she went on: "Anyway, I've been thinking about the qualities it takes to be a good parent. I used to dream about what the perfect father would be like. He should be patient, have a good sense of humor, be generous, friendly, understanding, and devoted. I'd like him to be honest, respected, and able to put the needs of who he loves above himself. I found that here. Age, really, has nothing to do with it. Because you're seventy doesn't mean you're going to die tomorrow, and because you're twenty-two doesn't mean you have fifty more years ahead of you.

"So, that brings me to this. If you will allow me to read the same as Captain Nedrick did, I'll let my writing do the rest. I think," she added with a giggle and a quick inventory of the faces around her, "That you're going to feel the way I did two weeks ago in just a few seconds!"

Junie laughed, patted the admiral on the arm, and then opened the folder she had brought. She read aloud in a clear, casual tone.

"_Number One_: I agree to give birth to one child fathered by any of the MS's that have signed their names at the end of these pages. These MS's will now be known as the Participating Male Subjects, abbreviated PMS's.

"_Number Two_: I will make every safe and natural attempt to give birth to a male child, but no matter what the gender is of the baby, the child will have the same rights, advantages and emotional devotion.

"_Number Three_: These children will be conceived in this manner only: From the signing of this contract, each PMS will have a twenty-four hour period with me in turn until I have become pregnant. The PMS's will be scheduled according to their military rank. Sexual intercourse, or the BT, will take place from one to three times during this period, and only after making an appointment with me with my consent. I will be fully prepared for the PMS's arrival, and I require each PMS to be prepared for his duty as no aid to his chore will be done by me. I will be as fully dressed as possible, without any predisposition toward seduction.

"_Number Four_: There will be no medical testing during my pregnancies unless ordered by my obstetrician. After the birth of the baby, the father will be identified by three tests, the same test or something different, so that fatherhood is never again in question.

"_Number Five_: After finding out that a PMS has a child, that man drops out of the rotation and the PMS's without a child will take their turns as before. Each PMS will agree to medical testing to determine they do not have any communicable diseases prior to the start of every rotation they take part in.

"_Number Six_: I will not ever give up my parental rights to any of my children. Custody will be shared equally for life. I will always have an equal say in raising my children.

"_Number Seven_: I will not accept any money as written in the previous document. I will ask for a small room in the PMS's residence in order to make scheduling BT's more convenient. I request that my medical bills and cost of living be divided equally among the PMS's.

"_Number Eight_: After the conception of a baby, the BT's will stop. After the birth, I will breast feed for three months, then I will have one month to rest and prepare for the next rotation of BT's.

"_Number Nine_: Every PMS will be an active and responsible parent to their child and to the half-siblings of their child, which will be considered their extended family, and they will be called Uncle by these children.

"_Number Ten_: After finishing this contract, I will move out of the residence of the PMS's. The children may remain with their fathers with the advantages their fathers can give them, and I will live as close to my family as possible. I will have as many rights and visitations as before.

Junie sighed, and then glanced up from the two pages scripted in black ink. The admiral had tears in his eyes, and he reached for her hand. To her left, Lieutenant Harvey was watching her in obvious astonishment, and to his right, Major Downs was looking at the floor with widened eyes, rubbing a shaking hand back and forth through his hair. Captain Nedrick was blinking while resting his head, and Junie had to laugh when spotting Colonel Harrison. He was to her right beyond the admiral. He had taken the same cloth she had used to wipe the paint from his chin and put it over his entire face. He was so slouched in his chair that it appeared he had fainted. "Colonel, are you all right?" She giggled. He merely raised both hands and dropped them again.

Admiral Crimmins gave one loud wrenching of the horn, and it startled everyone but himself and Junie. "Get a grip, men! What is this I see? Shell shock? Harrison, man, you were even a POW in your time! What were you doing in Manila, Hezekiah, working on your tan? I think not! This is the opportunity of a *lifetime*, men! Of a lifetime! We won't be just old coots living together, we'll be a *family*! Hand over that paper, Princess Ensign Junie! Point me to the dotted line!"

She squeezed his hand and laughed. "No, I don't want you to yet. If there aren't any questions now, I want to give you time to think about it. If you say you want to do this, you can call me. My daily schedules and all my work numbers are listed in here. I'll give it to Captain Nedrick. I also had the examination you asked for. Dr. Steinmannis now my OB/GYN. He gave me a thorough physical a few days ago, and he wrote up a paper that says there's no reason to believe that I wouldn't be able to fulfill this contract, and that I'm as healthy as can be. I didn't explain the entire thing to him, but I trust him and if we do this, I'm sure he'll be great about it.

"Are there any questions from any of you?" She glanced around her again, and still had to giggle. "Well, then maybe I'll go and you can all discuss it. I hope I haven't offended anyone. It's voluntary, you know! If you are uncomfortable, please forgive me and don't do it. The way I see it, you all have the means to hire someone at some point if you become determined enough. Like the admiral said, I would like to make a family instead of just an heir. It would be better for everyone this way, but especially the children.

"And I'm not offended about you all wanting boys,

either. If a group of single women all decided they wanted daughters, there would be no outcry about that, so I don't see why I should mind you wanting sons. It's even quite natural, perhaps!" Junie looked at the admiral and laughed.

"When you've decided, or…" she mentioned, glancing again at the colonel who hadn't changed his position, "recuperated, you can give me a call. I work three jobs and I'm hard to reach at my boarding house because I'm not there except to sleep at night, so even if you took a couple of days to decide, we couldn't start for a few weeks. I also want to say that if you sign and change your mind, that's fine. I don't know how much of this is legal, anyway, but as long as we understand what all this is about, we can do a good job at it. I'll go now. I had another great night with you all! Thank you very much."

Junie went over to the captain and gave him the folder. He accepted it without any reaction, unable to look at her, and rested it in his lap. She then went over to Colonel Harrison, lifted the cloth, and gave him a kiss on the forehead as she giggled. She replaced the cleaning rag. The admiral took her hand and escorted her to her car.

"I should drop the ensign now and just call you Junie, my dear," he said as they stopped on the patio.

Junie smiled down at him. "I've grown very fond of Ensign Junie, but I guess things will change a little bit with this, won't they? Do you think I hurt anyone's feelings, sir? Was any of that horrible? Captain Nedrick told me that you all had thought about it very seriously. I didn't get that impression just now."

He nodded, patting her hand. "I've brought it up many nights. When I met Rodgers and knew he had a mind for legalities, I admit it was part of his appeal to me. When we hit it off and I knew I'd invite the hobbler to come live here, I opened the discussion one night, and we all dove in. The work was done between him and me, but the others were keenly interested in it for their own sakes, too.

"You've laid a red carpet to the future, Miss June Bernice Smith! A beautiful, loving, red carpet. If only for myself, I would like you to give notice to all your employers and boarding house, and consider this your home whenever you are ready to come. Since you're not asking for any amount of money, we will give you a stipend you agree to. Please find this acceptable. I really don't know what they'll do now that they really can, but I'll make it known I am going ahead with it. The boy will type it up and do what he thinks should be done. What can I say to you, dear? Thank you isn't going to be enough."

Junie bent down to put her arms around his shoulders. "That you should be my close friend and the best father you could be to the child we may have is all I can ask, sir. Good night, Admiral Crimmins."

She kissed him on both cheeks, and he waved and tooted the horn until her car was well past the gates.

Section Five: Conception Roulette

Junie zipped the last suitcase closed. "There!" She took a deep breath and exhaled long and loud. All her packing was done. She had received the official invitation, and the guest suite at 60 Pond Point Avenue was awaiting her. She had fulfilled her obligations to her former employers, resigning with ample notice, but without explanation. A few had given her gifts or a party, and all had wished her well. Everyone wanted to know what she was embarking on.

"Oh, nothing much," she spoke aloud as she scanned her small bedroom. "I just have a standing date at our local birthing room nearly every year because I might be having five children with five different men, that's all! We're giving new meaning to the term 'business transactions'! Keeping up with my appointment book will be the first miracle, but the real thrill will be going to the Parent/Teacher conferences with five 'old coots' in uniforms. I hope no one is taking a sip of their coffee when we walk in! Oh, what Christmas card pictures we'll have!"

She had giggled as the words tumbled out of her mouth, but when they registered, she reeled and had to flop down on the bare mattress. Her eyes and mouth gaped. Captain Nedrick hadn't given any details when he called to voice the acceptance, but she had a silent wager with herself that perhaps two out of the five officers would have signed their names to her version of the contract. "Perhaps it's a good thing I don't have parents to explain this to! Do I really know what I'm doing?" she asked herself with another sigh. She imagined a few responses and was coming to a gentle laugh when there was a knock on the door.

"Junes? It's me."

She grinned. "Come in, Greg. It's open." She got to her feet and brought the suitcase to the door.

"Hey, Junie," he greeted, now in a soft cast. He glanced at her three articles. "This is it?"

"This is it," she answered with meaning.

They both looked down at the large suitcase, a smaller one, and a box full of odds and ends. Her room had come furnished, and she was allowed use of the house kitchen and utensils for her meals as she wished. Her bathroom was shared with the other boarders on her floor.

Greg shrugged, studying the items. "If you take the box, I can get the other two." He was surprised they weren't heavier. She picked up her share. "Are you sad, Junes? How does it feel leaving here?"

She looked back into the small room and grinned. "The owners and my neighbors were very nice, but I wasn't here enough to really be friends. It was lonely sometimes. I'll like it over there, Greg."

He repeated the shrugging, but added a sniffing noise. "I'll say! Do they have a pool? I bet it's an indoor one with all sorts of naked marble statues standing around it." They began their walk to her car, and she laughed for his misunderstanding.

"No, just shark-infested waters!" Junie laughed at his confused glance.

She had been told by Admiral Crimmins to sell her car, for she would have free use of his as he was unable to drive. She was giving her car to Greg. His hobby, for the time being, was mechanics, and he had eagerly accepted it in exchange for helping her move her belongings. As she shut the door behind her, her life changed.

The stairs were dark, stained, and narrow. Their footsteps echoed, and coming out into the sunlight made them both feel better. "Well, don't let them make you work too hard," he said, and Junie laughed again. Like the others, Greg believed she was going to become a live-in secretary. She didn't expect much contact with anyone she had worked for or with again, so the truth would never fully be known. "You're a good egg, Junes. I'll miss you."

Her belongings were placed in the trunk. "You're not so bad yourself, Gregory," she replied with a smile. "Thanks."

The drive was twenty minutes, and she said little along the way. She watched the surroundings of the route change as they went into her new subdivision. The trees were full and green, the sky a clear blue, and different bushes were neatly blooming a rainbow of colors everywhere. The gates of the house were open for them, and she smiled at the fountain.

"Are you still going to order pizza? Maybe I can see you then," Greg asked as he whisked in and stopped squarely in front of the patio. Junie had always parked past the entrance so the automobile wouldn't obstruct the beautiful view.

She smiled. "I hope so! Get that ankle better, Greg, so I can see you every month."

They got out of the car, and Greg took the time to look over the façade of the stately Federal. He was impressed for the first time. "Wow, Junes, if they need more help, give them my name!"

She laughed. The door opened, and Admiral Crimmins came out. "Princess Ensign Junie has arrived! And with her is Gregory, the other fine young delivery man! This is the best delivery you'll make in your life, son! How are you, lad? Ankle healing on schedule?" He came to Junie and held one of her hands and kissed it. She put her free arm over his shoulders, and they faced Greg side by side.

Greg frowned. "Good, General Klink. How are all you old war guys?"

"The tanks are tuned up and ready for combat, Gregory! How many do you think the allies will sink today?"

He rolled his eyes at a highly amused Junie. "Almost all of them, General. Be careful. They're mad because we beat them last time. I don't think you'll survive this one." He made a face at Junie as he opened the trunk. She came over to help him. He whispered: "Junes, if you want to change your mind, I'll take you back and even give you your car without being mad or anything!"

She laughed and patted him on the back. "I'm fine, Greg, but thank you very much. You said you know how to transfer the title on the car?"

"Yeah. No sweat. Thanks, Junie. Thank a lot."

"Go ahead and do it. Let me know when you want me to come by the restaurant and sign. My room is just up the stairs, they said. Come on. I know it's your day off, and I don't want to take up all of it."

When they turned around, the four other officers had gathered with the admiral. "Whoa!" Greg responded, surprised at the bunch of them. "Junie, I think you're crazy!" he said under his breath as Major Downs came to help. He was passed the smaller suitcase and Colonel Harrison stepped over to take the box. "You shouldn't have quit your other jobs, I'm telling you! It's hard to find work in this town. Plus, none of them look like they've got more than three months left!"

Junie giggled, and thanked Lieutenant Harvey as he took the large suitcase. Greg shut the trunk. "I guess that's it!

Thanks, Greg. I'll see you sometime." She held out her hand.

He openly frowned at the five awaiting her as he grasped it. "Take care, Junes. I hope you're happy. This is a big deal."

Junie paused for the profound sentence, and then smiled. All she needed to do was turn and look at the company behind her. They each had grins on their faces, and she smiled the broader. They were a handsome, welcoming bunch, and she felt her growing affection for them. "Thanks, Greg. Keep Tony and Alberto in line. Learn the Heimlich maneuver! You never know when it might come in handy!" She laughed and hugged him farewell.

He raised a palm to the men, and got in the car. For the last time, the old brown auto exited the gates.

She turned to them. "Well, here I am!" She smiled with a heavy sigh. She bit her lip with a happy anxiety.

They smiled in return. "We're going to have a celebration tonight, my dear!" Admiral Crimmins announced coming forward to take her hands, as was his favorite way of speaking to her. He liked to see her smile down at him, and she always did. "You go get settled. Take all the time you want. One of the men will come and get you for dinner, if need be. Take a few days to get acquainted with your surroundings. Nedrick wants to speak with you about the last formalities, so how about if the others take your things up, and you two go over the little bits of this? I'm very glad to have you here, Junie. If it all stopped here, I'd still be the happiest man alive today. Welcome Home."

Junie looked at the others, feeling suddenly emotional, and then bent down to kiss him. "Thank you, sir. I'm very glad to be here."

Captain Nedrick led her to his office as the others allowed him the time he needed to mount the staircase. They went in, and he spread the contents of a folder out on his desk. "This is a typed copy of what you wrote, Miss Smith. It came to a page and a half, as you can see. Would you like to read it?"

"I don't think it's necessary, Captain, but thank you. It looks very...official, doesn't it?" She grinned at him, the reality occurring to her.

"These are your copies of everything. I have the originals here on file. If you will sign on the first line on the last page, I'll copy it and I'll give you your folder."

She saw the second page, and gasped. She looked up at him. "There are five names here! *All* of you signed?"

He nodded. "We thought about it until I called you. There wasn't much doubt about it, though you were wise in allowing everyone time. Every decision was made calmly, and after great thought."

"Oh, my," Junie breathed. She turned from his desk and went before one of the windows. She looked out over the side lawn.

Captain Nedrick frowned, considering her. "Miss Smith, is everything all right? I can see this has surprised you. I'm sorry. Perhaps I should have been more informative over the phone."

"Oh...don't apologize," she insisted with a shaking of her head. "No, this was my offer, after all. I didn't know what to expect, to tell you the truth. I knew I shouldn't judge from your reactions when I did my reading because I certainly changed my answer, didn't I? But I'm glad for this. I really am. This way no one is left out and it will be a wonderful, complete family of very good friends. We'll all watch out for each other, which is my main goal. And yet, Captain?" She turned to him.

"Yes?" He came from around the desk and stood beside her.

"I'm a little curious. Once we get going I know it will be all right and I don't think we're doing anything wrong, but…well, I wonder if anyone is as nervous about this as I am?" She winced and sounded a short giggle.

Looking at her, he had to grin. She stood out well against the darker colors of the room and her eyes were sincere and bright with the emotion and light coming in from the windows. "Actually, I'm glad you asked that, Miss Smith. I wanted to give you a little information off the record.

"There has been very little said about anything, and that surprised me. We have a very good rapport as a group, but perhaps this is something men wouldn't talk about. Or, the lack of communal conversation about this may speak volumes. I'm not sure how to look at it. Whatever, the decision about signing was made freely, and that's what counts. After a day or two of complete silence, I told everyone they could discuss their acceptance or refusal with me privately, they could write it down and slip it under my office door, or they could sound it out loud. Every avenue was open. But, until the day I called you, no one but me had any idea that there were five names on this paper. We all knew about the admiral, of course, but no one discussed it between each other until notifying me.

"And yet, you asked me to be honest and I will. Miss Smith, to put it delicately, I would say there isn't a man in this house who doesn't have his fingers crossed." He chuckled, and she smiled with him.

"The admiral, as you would expect, is very determined," he went on. "Downs will be his usual flippant self, which I don't want you to take offense to, and Harvey and I worry, yes. We worry most about you, truthfully. We want you to feel you're respected and deeply admired for not only what you're doing, but how you've thought to do it. I've thoroughly contemplated your contract and I see your reasoning behind every step. The admiral and I can't hold a candle to you when it comes to compassion, obviously.

"Harrison, on the other hand, has been more verbal. Miss Smith, he is completely, totally, and absolutely consumed with terror." He laughed, though kindly.

"Terror?" Junie reacted with a curious grin.

Captain Nedrick went back behind his desk. "He's a very quiet man, Miss Smith. Admiral Crimmins has known him for a great many years, and he doesn't know of the colonel ever dating once. From how he sounded to me, if he has dated, it hasn't been in my lifetime. Suffice it to say he's very shy."

"He signed his name, though," Junie commented, coming back to pick up the page.

"Yes, he did. And he was the first to come to me, I'd like you to know. He even beat the admiral to my door. He'd be an excellent father. His temperament is the ideal. He has a good head on his shoulders, and I look up to him. I wish him the very best," he gave. "There may be other pitfalls at first, but I have every confidence you'll be able to handle anything that comes along. There isn't a man here who isn't willing to help, so just keep that in mind. May I put in the firmest of tones that I am not worried about the character of anyone involved in this."

Junie smiled at him. She took a pen from a container and saw the one empty line. She signed her full name. "Well, Colonel Harrison will be glad to know that I'm going to be shaky, too, at first! And if it makes it any easier for him, or anyone else who has their fingers crossed, my doctor told me how to 'make my internal environment significantly conducive to conceiving progeny of the male gender', and it doesn't require acrobatics or boots or uniforms or anything like that." She laughed.

Nedrick chuckled and agreed. He put the page in a manila folder and tapped it on the top of his desk to line the contents neatly. "Good luck to us all, Miss Smith, and we thank you." He offered her his hand.

She accepted the folder and handshake. "At dinner tonight, sir, I'm going to request that everyone start calling me by my first name. That will help our edginess, I hope! Try saying it once to get used to it, please, Captain."

He flushed, and then said: "Your room is around the corner. Let any of us know if you need anything. The colonel said he'd be more than happy to help you redecorate if you'd like. I'll see you tonight at dinner. Junie." He smiled.

"Bravo, sir! Thank you, Captain. I'm sure everything will be fine, like you said."

He watched her round the open stairway and put her hand on the closed door of her suite. She looked back to him, and he nodded with a grin to confirm her room, and he went back in his office and shut the door to give her privacy.

Junie stepped in. As she hoped, the room was beautifully comfortable. The balance of dark details and light pastels drew her in, and she smiled with joy at all the flowers the major had placed in different vases for her. It was wonderfully airy, and someone had opened the balcony's French doors. A breeze played around the room, and she shut the door behind her to relish it. On the coffee table was a fruit basket for her.

In her parlor there were two sofas, two comfortable chairs, a television, a record console, and large windows with laced curtains dancing by the double-hung panes. The carpet was detailed with a colorful sculpted design, and she wanted to take her shoes off and wriggle her toes in it. She gasped with added delight when seeing the very painting the Colonel had promised of the gazebo featured on a wall.

Her bedroom and bath had new linens with a decidedly feminine pattern, selected specifically for her. The rose print on the comforter reminded her of the major's blooms, and beside the bed, on both night stands, were large vases full of just that. She went to smell them, and closed her eyes. Her anxiety was dissipating. They were welcoming her, and she would revel in it.

Their patterns began that night with their daily shared meal. Breakfast fruits and juices would be prepared by the lieutenant and left in the refrigerator, each waking and serving himself as desired. Each party gathered their own lunch from the supplies in the kitchen; these first two repasts being very informal and almost haphazard. Each evening, the lieutenant would serve delicious courses, and Junie began jogging or walking to wear off the lavish foods she was unaccustomed to.

She was a young woman who had earned her living by working hard, and coming into a home where everything was done for her and where she didn't have any outside obligations was at first a treasured spoiling, then a problem. The officers were paying her way, and she wanted to both occupy herself and be of service to them. In this quest, she gently took more of a part in the household and their lives.

Admiral Crimmins love to read, but his eyesight was failing him and even large print was difficult for him to decipher at times. Junie began reading aloud to him. After helping the others clear the table after dinner, or during the afternoons, they would take their places in the parlor or the gazebo and she would read as he listened with great appreciation. Often he'd close his eyes and as she progressed, the fire would be lit, the lamps turned on around the room, and the men playing cards would not only keep their voices down, but listen as well.

Colonel Harrison gave her a thorough tour of his library, and showed her a large tapestry he had designed for it but didn't have the skill to embroider. Junie had some experience with this hobby, and she offered to attempt it for him. She began one night between readings to the admiral, and then when she wasn't reciting, she took the materials out of a large sewing box and sat in her chair, hearing the men talk over the daily news or debating politics.

Major Downs was a disorganized person, and she helped him categorize the files he had kept about his plantings and experiments with his blooms. He bought a camera and they took pictures and made a series of scrapbooks with all his notes, and she learned more about these forms of life than she'd ever guessed she'd be exposed to.

Captain Nedrick was orderly in every way. The aid he needed, however, was not like the other men, and Junie had known this before becoming friendly with him. He was depressed about his health, and so to draw him out and do what she could for him, she began inviting him to walk with her. It took several weeks of polite summonses, but finally one afternoon he accepted because of the ridicule the others had increased in giving him. Their distances were very limited at first, and she was careful in extending it over time so not to hurt him and make him feel a success.

Lieutenant Harvey's joy was his own work in the kitchen. She asked him to teach her a few basic dishes, and it soon became habit for her to do the more mundane chores for their meals. It wasn't unusual for anyone to come into the kitchen and hear them laughing as she peeled, chopped, or diced, and very often the kitchen island—the very place she had met them—became the focal point of the house where anyone with an idle moment would gather, serve themselves a drink or a snack, and pull up a stool and sit and join in the conversation. They had become a family before any child had been conceived.

When she felt content with her living situation, Junie discreetly went to each man to discuss their appointments for the first rotation. They chose their time of the twenty-four hour period, and she wrote it on her calendar, and on a slip of paper. The officers initialed both, making it feel official. The slip of paper was then given to the officer as his reminder, and he'd put it in his pocket. All of this was supposed to be done in total secrecy, yet it became an amusement to her and the others when the man with the upcoming appointment would attempt confirming his time. The paper, usually folded into the smallest square possible, would be taken out and glanced at as if it were information from a high level, and then the paper was quickly stuffed back into the shirt or trouser pocket.

Junie would hide her smile when she'd see this happening, and Major Downs would give a mild teasing that could cause the other man embarrassment or upset. Captain Nedrick looked as if he might come to blows, and Colonel Harrison forfeited a card game and left the parlor after an exaggerated wink. Junie knew the major did so without malice, but she asked him to cease on behalf of their friends, and he did with difficulty as his sense of humor was more like the admiral's. The admiral would treat the date with respect, but would throw the slip on the card table or the bar and retire early for the night and tell them not to bother him during that time frame the following morning.

Because of the preparations Junie had to make, it was decided they would meet in her room except for Admiral Crimmins. She would go to him at the appointed time, letting herself in without a knock, and the door would be shut and locked.

Thus, six weeks after she moved in, the first rotation began with Junie preparing herself, dressing comfortably, and quietly going down the stairs to meet the admiral in his private quarters.

A knowledgeable Downs elbowed an informed Harvey. They were sitting at the top of the stairway that went to their floor. The admiral had made no secret about his appointment, and they had found it impossible not to watch her depart. "I don't know whether to say 'Let the games begin!' or "Gentlemen, start your engines!', or "And… They're off!'" he whispered and chuckled.

The lieutenant frowned at him. "I'm glad I wasn't in the army with you, Downs. You'd have gotten me into a world of trouble! I probably would have been dishonorably discharged." He was not particularly proud of where he was, but he found the summons irresistible.

Major Downs thought it too humorous. "Oh, come on, Harv! You've got to see the funny side of this! One day she's delivering pizzas, the next she's delivering our five children! Think about it! Only in America."

He sputtered: "I cringe to think that my son will have your son as a brother! I almost didn't sign for that reason!" he added with a pout.

"Go on! It's his honor and great fortune, Harvey."

The lieutenant had to smile. "I just hope my boy is older than yours so he can beat him up all the time." He chuckled.

"Think again! Undoubtedly, my son will be the first and your little runt will be the last, so instead of greeting him in the delivery room with a proud smile, tell Junior Harvey to start running!"

Harvey tsked him and shook his head. "What would you say if I told you to put your money where your big mouth is,

Downs?"

He looked at him. "What?"

"Who do you think will be first?"

Downs' mouth popped open. "And you worried about *me* being a bad influence? Saints preserve us, Donald, I didn't even *think* of making bets on this! But, I'll do it. Yes, I will. One hundred bucks says Alan Taft Downs, Junior, will be born in less than a year."

"You are so full of yourself!"

"Am not!"

"Are so!"

He mocked deep insult. "Am not, Harvey! All right, what's your bet, as if I'll be surprised?"

Harvey nodded calmly. "You will. I'll meet your hundred, big guy, and say the old man's up before anyone."

"Crim?"

"Shhhh! Harrison and Nedrick would kill us!"

Both grimaced at the fact and quieted. They huddled down and scanned the hallway before continuing. All was well.

"Are you nuts?" the major began again in a low, but still heated whisper. "I'd bet a hundred the old man never makes it out of his chariot!"

Harvey shook his head. "I take care of him more than you do, Big Al. He's pretty spry, and he wants this more than anything. He has for years. In looking back, we should have been shocked he didn't ask her that very first night. Where there's a will, you know. You've got to take that into consideration." He looked at his friend and nodded seriously.

Downs exhaled. "All right, then if we're handicapping, we've got other factors to consider. I'll put the old man in high contention, but that takes out Neddie and Harri

103

altogether. They'll have to tie for last. Nedrick has the faulty joints and Harrison…well, what does Harrison have? There isn't a female he hasn't peed in his pants in front of!"

Harvey scolded him once again. "I'd bet against you just to rile you, but I think you're right. Look at the set-up: We've got to do this at least once every five days to start with. I don't know if poor Harrison's got it in him to do it once a decade. But Nedrick's another matter. The guy hardly makes himself walk around the house, but even if he has trouble right away, he's got to have the edge over Harrison and maybe over all of us because of his age."

"His *age*?" argued Downs. "That nerd acts older than all of us put together."

"But, he's really only in his thirties, Downs. That's a big plus for him. Virility, you know. That's all that counts. Do you remember when you were his age?"

"Yeah?"

"How would you feel if you had guaranteed-in-writing chance every five days with someone like Junie back then? Even with the 'faulty joints', and you *want* to get her pregnant? Think about that!"

The major obeyed, and then gave him a heavy scowl. "Even though they're BT's, I wouldn't be walking by the time I was forty. Damn Nedrick."

Harvey blew out an agreeing sigh. "All right, so this is my bet. One hundred dollars that it's Crim, me, Neddie boy, you, and Harrison, if he's really lucky."

Major Downs hit him. "I see you've overcome the age gap, Stud Harvey!"

He smiled and bent over his knees to not laugh too loudly. "Some men are just superior at any age."

Downs had to calm down and smile at him. He shook his head as he watched the hallway. "All right, Lieutenant

Virile, mark these words: It will be me, you, Nedrick, the old man, and Harrison. Again, if he's really lucky. No matter how nervous I get, all I have to do is remember his turn was before mine, and I can beat my hairy chest!" He chortled.

The lieutenant frowned at him. "You'd better be quiet or I'll change my bet and put you last. We shouldn't pick on him. He's a good guy and he deserves it. That might even make him first! And these are BT's, you know. It isn't about anything like hairy chests. We're taking this all wrong. We're not being fair or respectful."

The major quieted again, and put his arm over his friend's shoulders. "You're right. This is about something far beyond any of that. I've thought a lot about it, haven't you? Since Junie read her contract, I've been picturing everything. I could have said yes with tears in my eyes before she left the driveway that day. I had given up, Don. What about you?"

He thought silently, and then nodded. "At fifty-eight? Retired? In this small town with only you guys?" He chuckled. "Yes, I had."

They were in agreement, and then shook hands to wish the other well, slowly turning their gaze to the stairway.

"Taking a bit long, isn't it?" the major wondered.

Harvey shrugged. "I just hope he tells her where his nitro-glycerin pills are or we might have to do it every four days!"

Downs sputtered a laugh with him.

Junie sat down on the Admiral's bed. "Sir? I'm here."

"Almost ready, dear! How much time do I have?" he called from the bathroom.

She tried to remember the instructions. "About fifteen minutes, Admiral."

The sound of the horn reverberated against the tiles. "Unfortunately, that will be hoards of time! Get ready! Here we go!"

Junie watched as the admiral burst through the bathroom door with nothing on his underweight body but a hand towel over his lap. Her eyes widened and she attempted not to smile.

Admiral Crimmins used all his strength to propel his chair to the bed, in which the wheels crashed against the frame and he pushed as hard as he could to catapult himself onto the foot of the mattress. Junie was sitting more than two feet away from him. She slapped a palm over her giggling mouth as he clutched the sheets to hold himself up as his legs dangled over the edge.

"Ensign!" he said with a moan, "Forgive me if this is rude, but this feels excellent already! I should have been doing this for years!"

The wheelchair rolled backwards and away, and Junie stood up to retrieve it, trying not to take in the sight of his naked backside. With a gentle slide, he allowed himself to occupy it again. She got the towel from the bed and covered him as she wore a humorous frown. "Sir? I think we have to try something else."

He sighed. "Quite naturally. If at first we don't succeed, as the saying goes. It does appear as if work is needed on my stamina. You may be correct in that a different approach is what's needed. I should have planned a second mode of attack. It's back to the bathroom for me, Ensign."

"Can I help you, Admiral?"

"It's greatly appreciated and I'm very curious, but no, you're not supposed to."

"I mean with returning to the bathroom, sir."

"That's where all the action has taken place so far, so I must refuse that as well, I'm sure."

Junie laughed. "You'll get it, Admiral. Let me give you

an encouraging toot on the horn, and I'll take you to the door." She stood, her oversized garment flowing loosely on her. She began to wheel him back to the lavatory after putting the horn to use.

He smiled for her attitude. "Courage, Ensign, that's the ticket! Give me a few minutes and out will charge the light brigade! My most heartfelt apologies about the light, but we might as well call it what it is. Many wars have been won with heart rather than with might! Perhaps before my next appointment I shall partake of a garlic special. I won't eat for two days beforehand, and I'll eat the entire pie in less than thirty minutes. I shall be aflame in more ways than one, is what I'm saying! I just may break a few records in the BT Hall of Fame! Spoil it for the other men, that's what I'll do, but I can bear the responsibility. Here are the facilities, so relax for a few minutes, then just watch out. Just watch out, I'm telling you! We'll give it another try for the honor of our great country, what do you say? That always revs my engines!"

"Aye, aye, sir!" She had to laugh.

Downs and Harvey elbowed each other with strength. Junie had walked by without noticing them.

"She was *smiling*!" Harvey gasped.

"Score one for the old man! Saints preserve us; he *is* going to be first!"

"Good luck to Harrison, then it's you, Downs."

"Maybe I'll have to borrow some of his nitro-glycerin pills!"

They laughed, and then went on to begin their day.

Section Six: Gestating

[END AUGUST THROUGH APRIL]

In their first rotations, Major Downs, Captain Nedrick, and Lieutenant Harvey proved themselves punctual, formal, and respectful. Successive appointments gave them a welcomed routine, and the initial scheduling for these men and Admiral Crimmins ended without flaw.

After a short and disappointing pause, a second series of appointments were made and embarked upon, with two rounds passing for everyone except Colonel Harrison. This kind man would arrive in Junie's suite dressed as the others in slippers and a robe, but he would sit on a sofa with her and talk for a few minutes only to excuse himself with embarrassment. Junie was never anything but understanding, though she felt it was time to attempt a conversation about it with him. She outlined what she wanted to say, and waited for an opportune moment. One afternoon, as she was helping Lieutenant Harvey clean the kitchen, she saw Major Downs helping the colonel install a hanging glider in the gazebo. When the major left and she finished her chore, she departed the kitchen casually.

Junie stepped onto the wood of the platform. "Good afternoon, Colonel Harrison," she greeted, smiling at him in the swing.

"Hello, Junie! Would you like to sit with me?" He invited her happily, patting the ample space next to him.

"This is perfect for the gazebo. I didn't know a swing could be put out here." She sat down and became comfortable. She helped him gently propel the wide cedar frame.

"I forgot we had it," he agreed. "We didn't put it up at all last year. I realized it was the middle of summer before I remembered. I know you like the gazebo, Junie. I thought you might like the swing, too." He grinned at her. The work had been done with her in mind.

She smiled and took his hand. She held it for a moment with both of hers, and then began. "Colonel, there is something I'd like to talk to you about. I'm sure you know what it is, sir, and this is the perfect setting. Please don't say anything just yet, though. Let me tell you this."

Junie paused, hearing the birds, and enjoying the view and perfumes of the garden that was now in its prime. The bees buzzed around them, but with the warm temperature and so much pollinating to see to, the insects were a perfect addition instead of a worry. She patted his hand.

"Colonel Harrison, I never suspected that I'd be living where I am now, or doing what I am. If I hadn't begun to know you all, I would even have called it wrong. But, I like it. I like it very much. I have five wonderful friends to finally call my family. I am very fond of all of you, and I hope you all like me, too. As a person, I mean."

To his mind, this wasn't a question. He immediately insisted: "Oh, we do, Junie. We do. I doubt if anyone would have signed that contract if we didn't feel that way." He turned to her, grasping her hand tighter.

Junie grinned at him, warmed further by his sincerity. "That's what makes what we're doing right and not difficult for me. We could have done it scientifically, but I didn't want it to be done that way unless it had to be. I'm hoping this approach makes us more attached to each other, and that can only be good for the children. We'll be unconventional enough as it is, and I wanted a foundation of deep trust there before they were born.

"Colonel, there are men who can do what they want, how they want, and where they want, at the drop of a hat. They boast about it, and that makes them feel superior. Some women think that's very appealing and they brag about it, too, maybe. But I think you and I are different. I think you and I view these things with more romance and meaning, and we'd prefer to have them that way.

"I want you to know that I see you as being a very romantic and gifted man. Just like your talent, you give your heart totally, and those who receive it are very, very fortunate. You will do this for your child. I know the way your child has to be conceived is difficult for you because you'd rather be deeply in love and then you'd be free to express yourself, but I want you to know that if the world had been different and it was just you and I in another place and time, I know there would be no trouble for you at all. That makes you extremely attractive, and men like you should never undervalue that. I don't hold the others with less regard, but I do admire what you are and how you see this. Colonel Harrison, I am very much looking forward to putting your child in your arms."

He had turned to look in her eyes as she spoke, and Junie reached over with a soft grin and wiped a tear that trickled down. His tender soul was at ease. "Junie? Is it my turn today?"

She smiled. "Yes, Colonel."

"May we? Now, perhaps?"

Junie stood up and took his hands. "Yes, sir. Shall we go in?"

"Please. And, thank you." He stood and led her hands to rest on his arm. He was at peace, smiling, and he calmly escorted her into the kitchen, past Harvey who stopped pounding the night's steak, and through the breakfast room, foyer, and around to the stairs. Admiral Crimmins was in the parlor with the other men, and Junie squeezed his arm and laughed with him as they heard the horn tooting and the major and captain stop talking. She opened the door to her suite and took him in. Her speech would prove this moving only once, but he was as confident as could be when meeting his fellow officers later.

During this time, she and the admiral finished their second book and started on another he borrowed from Colonel Harrison. The admiral preferred aged classics, heavy in drama, and she felt her own education expanding. The tapestry for the colonel was taking shape, and her cooking techniques had improved so much that Lieutenant Harvey stopped instructing her, and they become a comfortable team. Major Downs was having her take notes on a new grafting experiment, and then, one day, as she invited the captain to come walking with her, she took his cane from him.

He looked surprised. "Junie?"

"You don't need this anymore, sir. When we started out, you leaned on it and you were very slow. You did use it. But, yesterday we walked a good two miles and I was worried about keeping up with you! It's just a walking stick now. If you want, hang on to my arm, but I feel certain this can be put away until your next operation."

The captain's face clouded, and she came over to offer her arm with a bright smile.

"Please, sir. It's a beautiful late summer's day, and you can tell me when to turn around."

The others cheered for a loud minute, with Major Downs coming over quickly and taking the cane from his reach.

Junie laughed and clasped one of his hands to be tucked into the crook of her elbow. Lieutenant Harvey ran to show them out. Admiral Crimmins tooted his horn, and Colonel Harrison stood behind them and gave them a gentle shove.

Junie laughed, and kept him moving. The captain looked back at them and frowned, then warmed his expression in being persuaded by all of them.

"There! You see?" She kept them on the grass near the pebbles and headed them for the gate the major had opened for them.

"So you are right, Junie. I didn't realize it. I had become so used to having that in my hand..." He smiled and squeezed her arm, patting it with the other. "Thank you. Thank you, Junie, very much."

She smiled up at him and from then on made no allowances for his progression. The next day his fear was gone and he didn't need her to steady him, and they increased their pace and distance by comfortable lengths. She saw parts of the neighborhood she hadn't seen before, and when the leaves started to turn, they had three different routes to choose from.

They had invited the other three to hike down to the pond, and they did so, discovering a canoe outfitter who rented them two of his five canoes for an hour. The pond was larger than expected and pristine, and they enjoyed their date of a picnic lunch in the shade. The captain declared he was going to break out his long-stored fishing gear, and the colonel wanted to try with him. Junie would attempt it a few times herself, but she mainly enjoyed walking down to see them trolling or casting and waving to her from wherever they happened to be. The captain began to wear more leisurely apparel, and he didn't distance himself as much as before. He told them one night that as soon as the rotations were successful, he would schedule his upcoming operation so to have his healing over by the time the child was born. Even he had dropped the pretense of "heir". Junie smiled at him, very pleased.

They were as much a part of the others' lives as if they had no other history but years together. Each man had become a caretaker to the other and to Junie, and she to them. Not a sniffle went by unnoticed, not a problem unresolved by the six of them, nor did even the slightest break in relished daily habit go unrecognized. One morning the crowd of officers was in the kitchen pouring themselves their coffee when the admiral asked with great affection: "So, where's our better half, I'd like to know?"

Lieutenant Harvey smiled for having the answer. They had glanced from one to the other and saw his expression and settled on him. He shrugged with a knowing grin. "She usually comes down by seven and turns the coffee pots on, but when I saw she hadn't been here yet, I went up to her room and knocked on her door." He went to the refrigerator and looked to see what type of juice he'd like to have that day.

"Well, man?" the admiral demanded, perturbed at him for being so slow. Every face was turned toward him.

"So, I asked how she was, that's all." He chose his nectar.

"AND?" the major shot loudly.

Lieutenant Harvey chuckled. "She didn't answer. I knocked again, and she called for me to come in. So, I did." He went for a glass. He began to pour himself the juice.

Captain Nedrick slammed his fist on the counter. "Listen here, Harvey, if you don't finish in double time, I'll break that pitcher over your head!" He got many cheers of agreement for this, and even a toot from the horn. "It's not like her not be down here. We miss her! We have a way of doing things around here now, and we all like it this way! We can't start the day without seeing her and having her say something! You were coughing last night! She's got to come down here and ask how you are so we all know, for God's sake! What's going on?"

Harvey laughed, feeling it was true. "I don't know for sure because she was in the bathroom and couldn't come out."

"Oh, wonderful!" Colonel Harrison said. "We shouldn't mob her, you know. We shouldn't make such demands on her. With all the BT's and everything else we're having her do, it's a wonder she's not falling apart. Is it someone's turn this morning?"

They knew as they always did, and looked at Downs. He shrugged with a nod. "Not until after dinner."

The admiral tooted his horn. "On a full stomach, and toward the end of the day! I give you credit, lad!"

He smiled, straightening his collar.

Nedrick scolded both with a huffing noise. "Well, Harvey, did she say anything to you? Is she okay?"

He smiled anew. "I don't think so. She sounded sick to me. She was throwing up." He winked at Downs. "I think she might be eating pickles for breakfast from now on. I'd better stock up."

Captain Nedrick's mouth snapped shut and his eyes widened. Down's mouth dropped open and his eyes narrowed, and the admiral began tooting the horn a dozen times in rapid succession.

The innocent colonel was mortified at their reactions. "Are we heartless men? Admiral, for shame! What are all of you laughing for? This is terrible! Junie's sick, the poor dear. She probably got it from one of us. I'm going to go see if she needs anything, and I'm sure it won't be a pickle!" He began the way to her suite.

The admiral deftly rolled his wheelchair into his path. "Not so fast, Hezekiah! Don't rush the lady in the mornings now!"

"She'd better had gotten it from one of us!" Downs said, going over to Harvey and shaking his hand. "Maybe from you! You're the one with the cough!" They laughed together.

Kind Colonel Harrison didn't understand. "What do you mean? Are you being crueler than usual, Major?"

The captain had calmed, and he went to pat Harrison on the back. He smiled at the admiral, and then addressed him. "Sir, we're hoping Junie is sick only in the mornings. Do you understand?"

"How kind of you!" he responded sarcastically.

"Hezekiah!" Admiral Crimmins shouted. "Morning sickness, you BT dolt! Who gets morning sickness, man? You?"

He thought. "No."

"Me?"

"No, you're always very lively in the mornings, Admiral."

"Nedrick?"

He looked at him. "Not that I know of." The captain looked at Harvey and Downs and they laughed.

"Downs?"

Colonel Harrison frowned at the one who usually teased him. "Probably not," he said with a wishing tone.

"So that leaves Harvey, I suppose?"

The colonel opened his mouth to deny it, and then it was clear by his expression he had come to understand. His eyes began to protrude. "Junie! She has morning sickness? Do you mean… *A rabbit might soon be dead?*" He quietly gasped. Those surrounding him smiled broadly.

"My good man, not to wish any varmint ill, but let's hope there's a celestial pile of carrots being prepared for a bunny with Junie's name on it!" Admiral Crimmins responded with excessive noise on the bicycle horn. "Ah, the sound of little feet may well be pattering soon!" Downs and Harvey slapped each other's hands in an athletic style.

"I feel ill." Harrison groped for the counter, swaying, and Captain Nedrick laughed as he helped him balance.

"I think you'd better take that back, Admiral," he said, holding the shoulders of the older man. "I think our good colonel is going to have morning sickness, too."

They all laughed, and after Harrison was safely seated, they finished their breakfasts and cleaned up. It was difficult for them to see Junie for the next few days without appearing to gape. They were very anxious to inquire, but they decided not to, not wanting to put any pressure on her. She came down as usual the next few mornings, acting normally, and they sadly decided it was indeed Harvey's cough. Pickles were not ordered by him.

It was a month later as they were enjoying their dinner when Junie said: "I went to the doctor today."

The forks or glasses that were en route to mouths or the table froze in action. The men openly stared at her.

Their reactions both delighted and scared her. She took a deep breath, looking from one non-breathing body to the other. She bubbled over with a happy giggle.

"Congratulations, everyone! The six of us are pregnant!" She raised her glass, laughing at them. Tears came to her eyes as well.

The admiral reached for her hand, and she turned to him, her tears falling down her cheeks. She took his hand with both of hers.

"We're due the middle of May. If you all want, you can

come with me for my next appointment. I go back next month."

"Next month!" the colonel cried out. "Shouldn't you be going every day? No, the doctor should be *living* here!" He flopped back against the backrest of his chair.

Junie laughed and released the admiral. She turned her attention and affection to Harrison. "Colonel, we're going to have a wonderful, healthy, beautiful baby. It's all going to go very smoothly. Much later on we go every week or every day if we need to, but right now, God and Mother Nature are doing the work with just a little help from us. Are you happy, sir?"

He looked at her, and put his hands over her arms. "Yes, dear. I'm very, very happy." She kissed him on the temple, and he smiled at her.

In her joy, she went to the lieutenant and kissed his cheek, then to Major Downs who embraced her for his kiss, Captain Nedrick was happy to receive his, and the admiral couldn't let her go for a long moment. They raised their glasses for a toast, and life in expectation began.

As the weeks ticked by, the men boldly attended medical appointments with her. The looks they received in the waiting room didn't bother them. In November, Dr. Steinmann let each listen to the baby's heartbeat with his stethoscope, and it was all Junie could do to keep from laughing as she lay patiently on the table. Afterward, Major Downs immediately went to a medical supply house and bought each man their own instrument. It became commonplace to see a pair hanging around the necks of the men playing cards, tending the garden, working at a desk, or chopping in the kitchen. At first she obliged them, but even her patience wore thin for all the interruptions, so in less than a week, she collected them and put them aside for later.

They were openly disappointed.

Along with that, "Dear?" the admiral began as she came to sit beside him to read, "I was wondering when our fine, young person was going to start making him or herself be known. We are into our second trimester now, and I don't see any change in your attire."

She opened her mouth to answer him, and then realized each man had dropped what they were doing to turn and stare at her. She took the sight in, and had to laugh. "You had all better relax because we're not even half way there yet, and that's if the baby's on time! First pregnancies usually run late, Dr. Steinmann told us, so it might be even a little more than nine months! But, my regular clothes are tight. I'll soon be in maternity wear. Then you won't remember what I looked like before I was pregnant!" She laughed.

And it was true. Junie's wardrobe changed in another few weeks, and during a visit where Dr. Steinmann told them the position of the baby inside her, the men asked so many questions she had to only lie still and they would think of what she wanted to know. She laughed as all five put their hands over the area. When the baby moved they were startled, then even more attentive than before. She couldn't pass a single officer, nor could an officer pass her, without putting his hand over the baby, and she lovingly paused for this every time. She enjoyed it herself.

Her walks with the captain continued until the first snow came, and, right before the holidays, he told them it was a good time for him to have his second hip replacement. They all escorted him to the same military medical center where the baby would be born, and he woke in his room to see Junie napping in a chair beside him.

As was natural for any of them, he reached over and put

his palm on her growing belly, and smiled. Junie woke and saw him and grinned. "Captain, how are you?"

"Fine, Junie. How are you two?"

She was glad to put her hand over his. "We're fine, sir. Your doctor said this surgery went better than the other one. Did they do the worst side first?"

He nodded, still groggy. "Yes. I'll be bouncing around in no time, now."

Junie smiled. "Good! The major and the lieutenant are down in the cafeteria, and Colonel Harrison took the admiral to the nursery and delivery entrance. Again." She laughed.

Captain Nedrick smiled. "If that's the case, then I want to tell you something, Junie."

She grasped his hand, and he squeezed it. "What, sir?"

"I could speak for all of us, I know, but I'd like to say this on my own behalf this time. I am very grateful to be a part of this, Junie. It's meant the world to me. I love this child. I don't care who the biological father is, I'll take care of it and do for it without any regard to that fact. I know that's why you thought to have things this way, and no one except a person with a great deal of love to give could have thought of it. You've brought that out of all of us, Junie, and it's been a pleasure. I consider it an honor to be a part of the lives of any of these children. And if you should give birth to my child, boy or girl, it doesn't make any difference."

Junie got to her feet and stood next to him. She was cautious of the bed as she didn't want to move it and hurt him. She bent down and kissed his forehead. She smoothed his hair and fussed with his covers, grinning into the grey eyes watching her. "Look out, sweetheart," she spoke very softly, "you're in grave danger of not being called a stuffed shirt anymore." They smiled, and then she sat down again, holding his hand, grateful that he and the others felt the same way she did.

Captain Nedrick came home to rapidly heal with the visits to a physical therapist and exercises at home. Since he could no longer walk safely outside because of the advancing winter, a treadmill was purchased. Junie chose to do her laps by walking from the fireplace in the parlor to the farthest point in the kitchen. Back and forth she went the full length of the house, and the men watched her with a considerate eye. To always keep them involved, she'd have them count her trips as she walked by.

"Three, Junie. Ten of hearts, Downs, and I've got you this time!" Nedrick called out.

"You do not, Neddie Boy! I have an ace right here, and I think you're cheating anyway! Show what's in your pile, my friend, or die at dawn! I've been watching you since you won that last hand under suspicious circumstances, and I'll be darned if you—Four, Junie—take my ten spot this time!"

Colonel Harrison put down his baby book with disgust. Since the pregnancy announcement, he and Junie had been reading child care books and looking at pictures of a developing fetus every evening. Even the admiral had put away his classics and wanted to hear what was currently known about the gestational stages. "Do you men realize there are the ears of a young, impressionable child going in and out of this room? It says here that the sense of hearing is very keen, even at this age. Even minutes after birth, a baby will turn his or her head in the direction of its mother's voice, and I would hate to see the expression on this—Five, Junie—child's face if it had a reaction to what it's hearing from you!"

"Put a sock in it, Harri," the major said. "My child is not going to turn its head in any direction when it's born because it will be too busy looking at me, his or her Poppa! He or she will be smiling from ear to ear and throw his or her arms around my neck and cry with happiness for finally being with me."

Harvey laughed. "And unless he or she has a diaper on, he or she will—Six, Junie—show you his or her plumbing, too!"

Junie had to pause and laugh at that line.

With the Captain's recuperation going well, they collectively turned their concentration to yuletide decorations. From the first floor to the third, inside and out, the historic Federal was resplendent with wreaths, lights and bows. The white snow set off the display, and they chose the fullest tree available: one of seven feet in height. The men had never purchased a tree before, and so they filled two carriages with trimmings for it. It was posed proudly in one of the bay windows, and it enthralled the traffic on the avenue as well. The fountain had been turned off before Thanksgiving, but often Junie would come down the stairs in the middle of the night as insomnia touched her now and then. She'd sit in her Queen Anne and watch the lights twinkle.

One morning Lieutenant Harvey found her asleep in the chair, and she explained what often occurred. After that, if one of the men awoke also, they would venture down to see if she were there. They'd sit quietly, talking in low volumes, thinking about the near future. They would light the fire for her, too, and she enjoyed that very much. She was happy and healthy, and was a relished textbook case.

For Christmas, each expectant father gave the other expectant father an item of baby furniture. Junie had told them the baby would sleep in her bedroom until the following child was born. She had expected the men to put their cribs, playpens, swings, and changing tables in their spare rooms, but they set the array next to their beds and were happy to show her the arrangements when they finished. Her present was the gift of a van that could seat twelve. They had selected it together, and she both laughed and cried at the cavernous interior. Major Downs took a picture of it in the driveway with the huge bow wrapped around it. Her gifts to them were albums to record first milestones, announcements, report cards, and growth, and she also redistributed their stethoscopes to further their bliss.

With the men taking turns counting off each day of the next four months, Junie was grateful when Dr. Steinmann gave her the name of a birthing coach. She arranged for private lessons, and they looked forward to their first class with anxiety and joy. Captain Nedrick misunderstood and bought binders and pens for everyone to take notes. Their coach, Dianne, laughed and explained only a caring ear was necessary. In the first session they went over conception and the stages of pregnancy. Everyone was familiar with that and they covered this as if experts, but the next lesson exposed a problem that would take a length of time to resolve.

"You all are doing very well," Dianne said, putting away the last chart and diagram. "So now, it's time to graduate to the actual techniques we're going to use when Junie goes into labor. I'm going to need some pillows for Junie's back, and I'm going to ask that those who can get down on the floor with her do so."

"I'll get the pillows, madam," the admiral offered, and went to his suite. Junie picked a clear spot on the parlor floor and sat down. The others sat around her. She happily patted each thigh near her.

Dianne smiled. "I must say, this is the most unique

experience with coaching that I've ever encountered!" she spoke with a laugh. "When Dr. Steinmann told me about you all, I thought he was joking. I have coached for twenty years and have helped my two daughters give birth, but nothing is ever going to top this!"

The admiral returned with three large pillows from his bed, and two huge, fluffy pom-poms.

"Admiral!" Junie exclaimed, laughing. They all joined in.

"I can't get down there, so I'll cheer from up here. I saw these in the store the other day and I knew this was just what was needed! I'm not one to just sit around while someone else does the work, so I'll be rooting away, keeping the course straight as she goes! Quite naturally, they're striking in color and the sound effect is rather astounding. The next time I fall for a televised cheerleader, it really will be for her voluptuous pom-poms!" To their amusement, he demonstrated lavishly, pleased with himself.

"Just so you know, they won't allow those in the labor room or delivery room, Admiral Crimmins," Dianne said.

He hit his lap with them. "And why not, I'd like to know?"

"They're not sterile."

"I'll sneak them in!"

Junie laughed. "You'll look more pregnant than me! Admiral, we'll take a picture of you cheering. That will be my focal point." She smiled, not sure if she'd be able to keep a straight face even while in hard labor.

"We'll just see about that!" he decided, slightly angry.

Dianne directed them to put the pillows behind Junie's head and under the small of her back. "Labor begins with the first contraction, but it will be many, many contractions later that Junie will be allowed to push. In this meantime, you, as her coaches, will have to redirect her attention and instinct to bear down. She'll be in pain, gentlemen, and you'll want to do what you can to take her mind away from that, too. You'll distract her by having her consciously change her breathing pattern and follow you. Make a small circle with your mouth, and pant quickly like this." She demonstrated. "Now, all of you try it."

The admiral began, and so did the major, captain, and lieutenant. They all looked from one to the other to make sure they were doing it well, then their gazes stopped on Harrison.

"Colonel?" Junie asked, resuming the breathing.

"Colonel Harrison, please try. It will be important when the time comes," Dianne encouraged. She kept her eye on him as she reached into her instruction kit.

Harrison nodded, closed his eyes, formed his lips, took a single breath, and fell over in a graceful heap.

"Colonel Harrison!" Junie called, trying to sit up.

"Take it easy, Junie," the captain said, helping her up. "Harrison! What gives?"

Downs and Harvey were by him, shouting his name, patting him on the cheeks. The admiral shook a pom-pom over his face. The poor colonel lay very still, sprawled over the floor. Dianne came with the stick of smelling salts she had ready. "I can always tell. He's all right. He just fainted, is all."

"Fainted! And all we're doing is *breathing!*" Lieutenant Harvey huffed.

Junie laughed. His shin was near her, and she rubbed it with her hand. "Colonel? Colonel?" she called gently with a smile.

The salts were used, and he began to moan. Dianne shook her head. "I don't hold up much hope for this one, Junie. Every student I've had that's fainted at this point has never made it near the hospital, except if they became the patient themselves, which is highly probable."

"Oh, no. He's going the distance." Junie got to her hands and knees and crawled over to him. "Colonel? Colonel Harrison? Wake up, sweetheart. Look at me."

He did, sheepishly, and frowned. "What...? Oh, I...? Oh, Junie, I'm sorry!"

"Don't be, darling. If you want, just sit it out this time and watch, but next week you're going to be right beside me. We'll practice during the week, too. Are you okay?"

He straightened his shirt and glanced around him. "I'm fine. Please go on. I'll get my chair and sit beside Admiral Crimmins for now. Maybe he'll loan me a pom-pom."

The admiral frowned at him, and moved the pom-poms away.

"No offense, but if we continue this it might be best if you remained on the floor," Dianne commented. "Junie, back on the pretend delivery table, please."

"Oooooh..." the colonel said, and did stay where he was. Downs and Harvey laughed, and Junie patted his leg as she returned to her former position.

"I don't know if he's been reading too many books or not enough, but we'll find out and work on it," she said, and lay down with a watchful eye on him and laughed.

Despite having to be careful of one nauseous and unsteady father, the entire class graduated with honors. Dianne made them certificates, with a special award going to Colonel Harrison for his selfless effort. They had a party, and then all they could do was return to the countdown.

Section Seven: Progeny One

It was with great pleasure that Junie welcomed the splashing of the fountain in early spring, and that she and Captain Nedrick resumed their walks. This time it was she who needed a steady arm and more cautious pathway. Pink and white dogwoods were in bloom, and the bulbs Major Downs had planted over many years popped up with more color, they concurred, than before. Junie was going to Dr. Steinmann every week. Their due date arrived.

"This is perfectly normal," their guide told them all. "We'll let you go for another two weeks, Junie, and then we'll have to have a talk with this youngster. Go home and relax. Have a garlic special," he joked.

Mirth, however, became more difficult as the days advanced. Admiral Crimmins began grinding his false teeth. Colonel Harrison didn't tell anyone he was doing abstract. Major Downs was seen jumping up and down in a seedbed one afternoon. Captain Nedrick plugged in an extra piece of office equipment and temporarily disrupted the electrical system of the entire house, and Lieutenant Harvey appeared determined to break every piece of Irish stemware owned.

"This is Junie's fault!" he blurted to Major Downs who was watering the pots of herbs in the kitchen windows. He gritted his teeth over another shattered mess. "I dreamed last night that Dr. Steinmann said when Junie delivered they'd fill out enrollment for kindergarten, not a birth certificate! I don't know whether to order pickles, or not! I'm down to my last jar! I can't take this anymore!"

The major wanted to laugh. It was Donald Harvey eating the pickles, not Junie Smith. Her habits had only changed to suffering from insomnia. Yet, the joking couldn't come, for he had knocked over a ceramic pot of seedling rosemary before his friend had dropped the crystal.

They did what they could for her and Junie attempted to remain cheerful, but she had no choice but to feel as tired, heavy, and sore as she was. The kitchen stools were out of the question, and she missed standing or sitting at the work center with them. They moved to the small table by the windows for her, and when this became uncomfortable, Lieutenant Harvey chose simple meals for them to prepare together. During her reading to the admiral, she fell asleep in her chair, and the men who had given up their cigar smoking when it made her nauseated, now retired early so to ensure she rest. She'd kiss them all good night with her warm gratitude, and hoped she'd have cause to see them before morning.

A week past her due date, it was decided at dinner they should make a practice run to the hospital. She would announce the drill at the time of her choice, and they'd see if there were any flaws to be worked on before the true time. They were extremely pleased with this plan; the admiral going so far as to dub it *Operation Stork Cometh!* The men went to bed as if youngsters waiting for Christmas morning. Junie thought their confidence and giddiness so humorous she only waited until late the next evening to go to Colonel Harrison's room.

She knocked on the door. "Colonel? Colonel Harrison? Wake up, sir. Let's try the drill now. Wake up, Colonel. It's time to try *Operation Stork Cometh!*" She laughed.

Her humor, however, was the only one in continuation.

She heard a thump and a running from within the room, and the door was yanked open before her. "What? What did you say, Junie? Did you say it was time? It *can't* be time! We haven't had the drill yet! This is against military protocol, and who knows about the laws of nature!" He stood before her with his pajamas on, tiredness only slowing his grasp of realization, not the opening of his eyes or mouth.

Junie laughed and tried correcting the mussed, red hair. "Colonel, I'm not breaking the rules. Listen to me very carefully. *This is the drill.* It's *the drill*, Colonel. I'll wait downstairs and you can get the others up, okay? Please relax. I don't want anyone getting hurt tonight."

"Yes, Mr. President!" he shouted, and then slammed the door in her face.

Junie comically frowned then sighed, laughed, then knocked again. "Colonel, this is the drill. Please tell me you understand. *It is just practice."* She tried the knob, but the door had locked with the slamming. He sounded like he was running for his life in his own room, and more doors and drawers opened and shut than she thought he owned. She knocked again and called, but there was no answer.

She went to the Captain's room. The office was open, and she ventured to his bedroom door and knocked. "Captain? I need help. I thought we could try the drill now, but Colonel Harrison misunderstood me. He thinks I'm in real labor."

The door burst open, and Captain Nedrick tripped out past her into the hallway with a shirt on backwards, his trouser pants only on one leg, and one shoe on. He landed on all fours in the hallway. "Get up! Get up! Junie's in real labor! We need help down here! The Stork Cometh! The stork is operating and cometh on the second floor!" he bellowed through the still night.

"Oh, for goodness sakes!" she scolded, going to help him

stand. "You're going to hurt your hips again, Captain. Listen to me, please!" She helped him into his other pant leg so he wouldn't trip. He was trying to shove both his pajama top and his backward polo shirt he put over it into the waistline. "Captain, this is the drill, just like we talked about." He couldn't zip the fly, so she pulled the shirts out and did it for him. "Captain, I am not, *not*, NOT in labor. This is a *practice*, are you listening to me? Are either of you awake enough to understand what I'm—"

"Where's the President? I've got her!" Harrison had come running out of his room, and with the light on, Junie was able to see that she should take a step backward before he unavoidably cannoned into the captain. They scrambled to right each other. "I just packed my suitcase! I'll get the van! You get all the others! All five thousand of them!"

His miscount went unnoticed. "All right, Harr, good plan!" Nedrick began to run for the steps.

Junie frowned at them both. "Wait a minute! Will you two please...Colonel? Why did you pack such a large suit—"

"We're coming! We're coming!" Downs and Harvey slammed their suite doors and began stampeding down the stairs. "We heard everything! We're ready, let's—"

Downs, Nedrick, and Harvey all collided and came so near to falling down the wide stairway, Junie screamed and covered her cheeks with both hands. Every man stopped and stared at her, then gasped.

"Look at that face! It's hard labor, troops! There's less time than we thought! Hang on, Mr. President! We've got it under control!" Colonel Harrison shouted in panic and dashed over to help them, and the three sprang to their feet miraculously unhurt and went down with all eight arms tangled together.

"The Admiral!" Harvey yelled, rubbing his bruised head.

Junie looked over the railing to where they were standing and tried shouting over the din, but no one heard her. She tossed up her hands and walked calmly to the head of the stairs to descend. When she arrived on the first floor, she chose a safe spot and watched. Three of the men were in the admiral's room.

"Blast that, men! Take me naked if you have to, but don't forget my pom-poms!"

Junie had to laugh. She saw the front door was open and someone had enough sense to put the front patio lights on. Her van was being driven from the first garage. She wished to spare her vehicle any trauma, but in seeing a half-naked admiral being carried on Captain Nedrick's back, and Lieutenant Harvey pushing Major Downs in the wheelchair, she recognized the larger auto may have to be sacrificed for their lives. Her van pulled up on the patio, knocking over a large, ornamental clay pot, and Colonel Harrison pummeled the horn.

"Let's go, men! Stoke your courage, and let's show them how the United States military wins wars!" the admiral yelled, pointing the direction to be traversed with an outstretched arm.

Junie stood and went to observe them pile in, the admiral and his pom-poms be seated, the wheelchair loaded, and Captain Nedrick jump into the front passenger seat. Pebbles flew behind them as they took off. The van went all the way to the gate, skidded to a stop, paused, and then began a return to the patio in a squealing reverse gear. She began to laugh anew and stood in the doorway, waiting.

In front of the patio, Captain Nedrick opened his door and jumped out. "Can you believe it? We were going to let *Harrison* drive!" he said to her. "Junie, can you open the gate, please?" There was shouting, Harrison ran over to Nedrick's seat, and Nedrick ran to drive. Junie left only to go in the house to oblige him with opening the gate. More doors slammed, more yelling, and more pebbles were thrown back as the van started off again. This time it exited the property, screeching out onto the avenue.

Junie stood out in the night, looking at the mess made by the broken planter, and seeing the bricks the van's wheels had unearthed. She looked at the watch she always wore now for when her contractions did begin. "Nine forty," she said aloud. She went back in the house and shut the door. She pulled her Queen Anne to face the window, and sat down. She rested her head back, embraced the baby, and smiled. It was the perfect cure for her insomnia.

"Junie? Junie?" was the next thing she heard. She opened her eyes and looked up to see Captain Nedrick grasping her shoulder in the same outfit she had last seen him in. She raised her arm with the watch. "Twelve ten," she said out loud. She had to view it again. "Twelve ten? It's *ten after midnight*? What have you been doing! Is everyone all right? Oh, my, what is—"

"Junie, don't be worried," he gently insisted, then frowned heavily. "We're all right, as incredible as that seems. We didn't run over anyone, or lose any of us along the way, or put a mark on the van, or even get a ticket, though we certainly deserve something harsh." He shook his head at himself and the others with him. Crimmins, Downs, and Harvey chuckled.

"Then what took you so long!" she had to know.

Nedrick cringed, but knew the admission had to come. "We did have one little incident. Just a small one, Junie, nothing to fret about. We made it to the hospital just fine. Colonel Harrison, being the brave man he is, was the first to run into the emergency room. He shouted for a wheelchair, and when he realized we left you here, he… Well, he very safely and stylishly—"

"Went down like a truckload of dumped rock!" Downs finished with a flourish. "Arms outstretched to the max! If he had been diving in the Olympics, he would have scored a ten!"

Admiral Crimmins tooted the horn, and Downs and Harvey laughed. "Broke a floor tile, he did! It was a fine show after all! He got a standing ovation all around, quite naturally!"

Junie could only gasp and struggle to get up from her chair. A scowling Nedrick offered his hand to pull her up. "Oh, Colonel, where are you?" She saw the poor colonel purposely standing behind the others so the sight of him wouldn't upset her. The top of his head was wrapped in gauze bandaging. "Oh, sweetheart!" she cried, and went to embrace him. "My, my!" She laughed with empathy as she took his face in her hands and studied what she could of the injury.

"I'm all right, dearest. I don't have any stitches, and there's no concussion. We had to wait to be sure. We didn't call because we were hoping you fell asleep, which I guess you did. You told me it was a drill I don't know how many times. Wishful thinking, I guess. I just didn't pay attention. My last thought before I went to bed last night was if you really went into labor, you'd call it the drill because you wouldn't want to worry us and make us over-react. I'm so sorry, darling." He grinned sadly at himself as he held her.

"I'm more to blame," Nedrick commented with remorse. "I heard you, but I didn't listen, either. I'm sorry, too. I hope we haven't terrified you out of having us with you when the time comes, Junie."

Junie kissed the colonel, and he easily managed a relaxed

smile. "Of course you haven't! I figured if you didn't all kill yourselves tonight, I'm perfectly safe in your company." She laughed.

"Downs has offered me his flak helmet," the colonel added with his own laughter. "I'm going to take him up on it. Junie, I fainted for you this time, not for me! I was doing the breathing all the way there. All that practice paid off! I'm going to be fine and right there with you. This bump on the head was worth finding that out."

The horn blew again. "We were all doing it! Nedrick nearly hyperventilated, he was doing so well! Ensign Junie, or should I say, Mr. President, we're at the ready on full alert!" Admiral Crimmins declared.

She giggled, seeing him wrapped in a hospital blanket over a jonnycoat. She went to each and embraced them. "I'm so glad! *Operation Stork Cometh!* was a success after all. I don't think I'll do it again, but I'm glad you did so well. Why don't you set out your clothes before you go to bed, just in case? Make them *very* easy to put on. Tomorrow we'll repair the patio, and Major, thank you very much for lending Colonel Harrison your helmet. Admiral, let's take you in and get you warm, then off to bed for us all." She went over to take the handles of his wheelchair, but they protested. He tooted the horn for her cheering, and they sent her off to her suite with a kiss from each of them to her cheek.

Captain Nedrick put his hands on his hips when he heard her door shut. "I have never, in my entire life, been so humiliated by the actions of others, or acted so foolishly myself. I don't know if it was added stupidity we forgot to bring her, or if it wasn't the one blessing we had! There the five of us were with Harrison's suitcase, Downs' camera, two pom-poms, and no Junie!"

Downs laughed. "I would have gotten a great shot of

Harrison deep-sixing the tile if I'd thought to take the lens cap off!" He laughed with Harvey and slapped his back. "But hold on, Neddie boy! It's not even the big day yet! We might be even better, then!" He drew more serious, studying the camera hanging from a strap around his neck. "Hmm. I think I'll just take the thing off now," he mused, then noted his outfit: crumpled, twisted, with mismatched shoes. The chuckling returned as the protective cap went into his pants pocket. He began to take pictures of his friends, and they all had to smile.

It was Harvey's turn to laugh. His appearance was no contradiction to the others, and he put his arm over Harrison's shoulders in a mutual pose. "Should we tell her we were fighting over who was going to hold her hand?" He chuckled.

"Let's quit while she still wants us with her, men!" the admiral decided. "The less she knows about this foiled caper, the better, I say. Put that thing on the timer, Downs, and get in the frame! Make sure you get my outfit, especially the socks requisitioned from Harrison. Hezekiah, I hope you pack more than footwear when you take a trip, unless it's a nudist colony with cold floors that you're bound to! Rodgers, a fine back you have there, my boy! Carried me without a problem! Bless those new hips, also! Good thinking to put that shirt on backwards, the way you did. The V-neck gave me a handle to grip."

"Thank you, sir," Nedrick said in a dull tone. He had stumbled nearly seriously a total of three times and then toted the admiral across his arms to the van. In addition, the admiral's tugging at his shirt had given his skin a burn. He wasn't sure he was going to feel as well in a few hours, but he was smiling as the flash went off for the joint, affectionate portrait. Copies would soon be hung not only in each of their rooms, but in the parlor itself. Another professionally framed copy would be given to Junie.

With this, a new bond formed. They were more confident, and Junie's spirits were greatly lifted. The next morning, she inspected the outfits each made sure he set aside, and the admiral put his pom-poms on top of his.

Mercifully, thankfully, it was less than twelve hours later when she was reading out loud that the drill would prove more worthy.

"'And he cried from the mountain top---' Ooooow!" She made a groaning noise while putting her hand over her abdomen.

The admiral had his glasses off and his eyes closed. After a short pause, he said, "Junie, sink this new-fangled version! Moses never said 'Ooooow!' from the mountaintop in the old Old Testament! Charlton Heston would have looked like a dolt saying that in the movie! You're very good with the reading, though, dear. You sounded exactly like a moose. No fault on you. Men, did Moses ever sound like a moose in the bibles you grew up with?"

"I'm sure it's for modern realism, sir," Harvey said as he discarded. "Moses was carrying the tablets down. It was a sizable mountain and the slates were very heavy."

"What he needed were a few enlisted men to give Moses a hand," Downs said with a chuckle. "On the other hand, a relative of Harrison's might have been there and keeled over, so he might have said a lot worse."

"It depends if he could view what was going on since he left," Captain Nedrick added. "He did not return to a pretty scene. The dealer takes one card."

"He didn't say it," Colonel Harrison remarked, putting his book down with great haste, "Because he wasn't in labor! Junie, dearest, are you all right?"

She was staring at her lap. The admiral bolted upright, struggling to put his glasses on. The men playing cards dropped their hands and swung around so suddenly, many of the cards took flight. Harvey nearly toppled from his chair. Junie looked from one to the other, her own eyes expanding. "I might be wrong, but I think my water just broke. That had to have been a full contraction. Oh, my goodness!"

"Saints preserve us!" Major Downs breathed.

Junie sat back in the chair, willing herself to be calm, and she caressed the muscle that was beginning to do such work. The admiral reached for her hand, and she held it with a smile. "What shall we do? It's only six-thirty. We've got a long night ahead of us."

"Maybe we should go take a nap, dear," the colonel suggested. He departed his chair for her other side. He held out his hand. She looked to him and smiled, accepting it and the idea.

"That sounds good, Colonel, thank you. I don't think any of us are going to get much sleep tonight, so we'd better rest while we can. God willing, we'll be rocking a baby in our arms tomorrow at this time, so let's be ready for it." She giggled as she went by them, Harrison escorting her to the stairway.

"I'm going to rest and get my gear ready, men," he spoke as they passed them. "Junie will get us when it's time. Good evening Admiral. Fellow fathers." He happily nodded to them as he went up the steps, and Junie waved with a smile before disappearing from their collective sight.

The remaining four sat in complete silence, jaws gaping and eyes blank.

"The hell with him!" Downs reacted first. "The guy goes into a coma when we practice breathing, and goes off the deep end when we're only having a drill, and now that it's the real thing, *he's going to take a nap, for God's sakes?* I'm taking my damn helmet back! We need *someone* to be panic-stricken around here! I hate the guy's guts!" He pounded his palm on the table, knocking over the rest of the cards.

"Easy men, easy," Admiral Crimmins spoke. "There's no need to go off halfcocked. It will be a while, just like the lady said. We've known this was coming, and we wanted it to come, and we got mad when it wasn't coming, and now that it's here, *I can't believe I wanted it!* Nedrick! DO *something!* There is a woman upstairs about to give birth to our child, and we're all sitting here like a bunch of conscriptions! Save our souls! Man overboard! And where are my God-forsaken glasses, men?"

A frowning but sweating captain stood and went over to him. The admiral had put on his lenses, but upside down. He corrected them with shaking fingers. "I think we should do exactly what Junie and Harrison are doing. I can't think of anything more challenging, but we should at least lie down. We're not going to get any sleep otherwise, and we want to be in perfect shape to help her and the baby. And don't any of you let me forget her this time! God above, we've got to do this four more times! Is it worth it? I'll have ulcers by the time the third one is born!"

"That's right, five in total!" the lieutenant gasped. He began the breathing technique the birthing coach taught them. "I need a pickle!"

Downs laughed. "Remember, Harv? You didn't re-order!"

"Ahhhh!"

"Off to our bunks, men!" Admiral Crimmins called. They began to move out in slow motion. "Put on the clothes we picked out the other day so we can jump when Junie calls.

Don't toss around too much or we'll look like we did before, except for me, being practically buck naked means anything is an improvement. But change, shower if you must, and lay dead calm on your beds. Notify me when the moment comes. I won't be sleeping; I'll be lying down, holding my pom-poms. Off with you, you brave souls. Think like Harrison. Keep Junie's welfare at the forefront, and the baby, too, quite naturally. We'll pull through! I don't remember ever hearing of a man dying in childbirth, so we should be fine! Thankfully, these things are done in a hospital, so synchronized fainting spells are easily handled. See you in a few hours, men! Take heart! It will all come to an end!" He wheeled himself away with an "Oh, Gracious Lord, save us all! What happened to the good, old days when fathers could be out of the country when this happened?" muttered under his breath.

Downs, Nedrick, and Harvey took the steps in the same deliberate rhythm. They looked at Junie's closed door, glanced at each other with enlarged eyes, then parted with a weak salute. Downs and Harvey continued up, Nedrick rounded the railing. He stopped short when seeing Harrison leaning against his door, his clothing already changed into the chosen outfit, and a camouflage helmet on his head. The helmet came complete with artificial scrub. Green plastic branches stood nearly one foot in height above the protective wear.

"Colonel?" he asked. He waved a hand in front of the elder man's blank face. "Harrison?"

He swallowed, and then blinked. "I'm fine, Mr. President. I'm staying here. I'm ready. I'll take the first watch. When Junie blows reveille, I'll get the rest of you."

Captain Nedrick winced. "Colonel, the president is the one in labor, and that could be for some time. Is he—I mean, *she*—lying down now?"

"Yes. I put her in bed. I think. I'm not sure now, but wherever I put her, that's where she stayed."

Nedrick sighed. He stepped away and went to Junie's door and opened it quietly. The sitting room was empty, and he looked into the bedroom. She was lying down, on her side facing him, eyes closed and mouth grinning. He softened and calmed in looking at her. He returned to Harrison, his actions inspired by what he knew would be her behavior.

"Come on, sir, let's get you in bed." He opened the door and took him inside. He unsnapped the chin strap and removed the helmet from his head. He put it on the bedside table and led him to lie down. "Get some rest, soldier. We'll be ready and able. You did a fine job down there. You can be proud."

"Captain?" Harrison asked as he straightened his body over his bedspread.

"Yes, sir?"

"Did I tell you that when I went in the hospital and asked for a wheelchair, I meant it for myself, not for Junie?"

Nedrick grinned. "No, but it doesn't matter, Colonel. This time you can ask for her. Good night, sir."

"Good night. Please don't forget me, even if you think I'll get in the way. I promised Junie I'd be there, and even though I probably won't ever have a child, I want to be there as much as anyone else."

The captain patted him on the shoulder and left. He went to his own room, glancing first at Junie's door, and then went to change. He lay on the bed as still as a living soul could.

Junie dozed in little naps, waking with a contraction, keeping track of the timing, and getting up only to sit in a soft chair when she was no longer comfortable in bed. She called Dr. Steinmann and was told to wait until her contractions were six minutes apart. She checked the contents of her suitcase, blew a kiss to the awaiting crib, and went to Captain Nedrick's room.

"Captain? Captain Nedrick?" she called softly while tapping on the door.

He opened it, his face dark from needing a morning shave. He hadn't dared do it in case he missed her call. She smiled as she touched the roughness.

"It's not exactly time yet, sir, but I'd like some company. My contractions are regular, and about ten minutes apart. I thought if everyone wanted, we could sit downstairs until it's time to go. Is that all right with you?"

He grinned down at her, seeing how tired she looked. He straightened a lock of her hair. "Of course, Junie. Give me your suitcase. I'll take you down and then get the others." He extended his arm and she took it with both hands and a smile. "How are you feeling?"

She leaned against him. "Good, sir. I'm glad I have all of you." They took the steps slowly. He changed the placement of his elbow to put a tight arm around her and guided her carefully. The sun was just beginning to come up, and it lit the parlor for them.

"Sit in my chair, Junie. Put your feet up and relax as much as you can. I'm going to get the others and bring the van around. I'll put in your suitcase, and then we'll wait for you to tell us it's time, all right?"

Junie smiled. "Thank you, Captain. Take your time."

The others collected quietly, nervous, but thinking not of themselves this time. They did the proper breathing with her, joking for her, holding her hands, putting her feet up and rubbing her calves. When the contractions increased and came faster, she said she'd like to go. They put her in the front seat, locked in the admiral, and Captain Nedrick positioned himself behind the wheel.

The five of them checked her in and she waved a thumbs-up sign as she left to be prepared. In less than fifteen minutes, they were led to her room. Junie was slightly elevated in the bed, and she pointed to the picture the nurse had taped on the wall. She laughed. It was the admiral using his pom-poms, with what was supposed to be an encouraging expression on his face. They all smiled. The admiral rolled over to her side, Downs and Harvey took a hand, and Nedrick and Harrison rubbed the sheet over her ankles.

Her hair was beginning to mat from perspiration, and she was slightly pale, but they admired her appearance. "The contractions are three minutes apart, but I'm not dilating very fast. Here we go, is everyone ready?" She looked from one to the other as she began panting as she was supposed to. They all joined her, and the lieutenant took a cloth near the bed and wiped her forehead. She relaxed back and closed her eyes. "My back is starting to hurt."

"I'll rub it for you like we learned in class, Junie, "Lieutenant Harvey offered.

"Please, sir. Thank you."

Harrison was by the crank at the foot, and he used it to flatten her position. She turned on her side, and Harvey used his fingers to massage her lower spine.

"That feels very good. Thank you. Colonel Harrison, would you come over here in front of me, please?" She began to smile.

"Yes, love?"

She had to giggle as he squatted down in front of her face. None of them realized until that moment, the sixty-seven year old was wearing the loaned battle gear. "Excuse me, sir, but I just needed a little laugh. I'm so glad you're wearing that." She smiled, and he did also with a patting to her hand as she reached to examine the plastic branches.

"It seems to me they could do something for that," Major Downs said in an inconsistent tone. "How can we brag about putting a man on the moon when we can't even dilate a pregnant woman? This country has nothing to be proud of."

The patriotic colonel stood slowly and frowned. He kept Junie's hand. "Bite your tongue, sir. This baby's being born into the best country in existence."

Downs raised his eyebrows. "Fine for you to say, of all people! Wearing my helmet the way you are!"

Junie's next contraction interrupted them. She brought her legs up and the colonel brushed her hair back and rubbed her shoulder. Major Downs lost his frown and rubbed her legs. They all held on to her somehow.

"Listen, son," Admiral Crimmins spoke when it was over. "The most we can do for childbirth was done at the beginning of time. God Himself did it. He decided—in His infinite wisdom—that it isn't you or I on that table, it's *her*.

"Junie, dear, yes, I have commanded ships of all sizes, plotted a thousand courses, been responsible for millions of sailors in times of peace and war, and I do miss it. Along with the glory, I've seen men blown apart, shot, slashed open, burned, tortured, scream in agony, writhe in pain, pray to die, weep for their mamas, beg forgiveness, confess to every unmentionable sin, resort to eating bugs, suffer spasms of terror, pee in their pants, promise reformation, grovel like the lowest life form, or, in other words, express more than a mild desire to be doing something other than what they were doing at that moment, but never, ever did I hear of any of them yell they'd rather be contracting in childbirth. Good going, Ensign!" He tooted the horn as loudly as possible.

For such a speech, Major Downs stumbled over to the lone chair and collapsed into it as the others slapped their hands to their heads. "Saints preserve us!" he whispered, having to agree. He wiped himself with the spare cloth, and went so far as to start biting it.

"Use that on me when you're done, son," the admiral asked, sounding dizzy. "That was quite some stirring little talk I just gave, quite naturally! Better pass me the ice chips, next."

Junie could only sigh.

"Are you in much pain, Junie?" Lieutenant Harvey asked. "They can give you a little something, you know. Maybe we ought to have some." His eyes rolled. "I call it first!"

"What do you mean, 'is she in much pain?'" Colonel Harrison scolded him. "*Of course* she's in much pain! I had my appendix out when I was her age, and that was a little thing. Look at the size of this baby! She's been as big as a cargo plane for three months! I read the biggest baby ever born was almost thirty pounds. What if, because she's past her due date, she *beats* that? Would you like something almost thirty pounds and three feet long going through a small opening out of you? My God, of course it hurts! I can hardly stand it! Get that pain medicine in here and let us have some!" He stepped back and began to fan himself with a branch he tore from the helmet.

"They let Colonel Bush Head in here," the admiral declared with a pounding on his chair arm, "And not my pom-poms? And this establishment calls itself a military facility? Shame on them! Pass those ice chips, Harvey! Don't hold a monopoly, lad! I asked for them, fair and square!"

"I haven't had a pickle in five days! I need something to crunch on!"

"Downs, stop gnawing on that washcloth and give it to me to use on Junie!" Captain Nedrick said, seeing the need to go to her side. Downs tossed him the cloth, but the captain used it on himself first. He was the only one in any kind of shape to breathe with her.

Colonel Harrison was aimlessly walking about the small room, not concentrating on anything in particular. "Major Downs, I think it would help all concerned if you took back your comment about this country not having anything to be proud of because we can't dilate Junie by artificial means. As someone who has served tirelessly for the great majority of his life, I resent the implication that this beautiful land lacks deep inspiration. The fact that we can't produce humans by artificial means or the snap of your selfish fingers may be a saving grace of the entire modern world! You should be down on your knees in gratitude to your mother, Junie, and all women who do all sorts of horrible, tortuous things like this to us men!"

Junie and the captain were ignoring them and blowing into each other's faces.

When Lieutenant Harvey talked, small particles of ice blew from his dry mouth. "My mother had me by Caesarean. It was scheduled. She was completely out and my father was watching a rerun of the latest Army-Navy game in the waiting room. That's what I'm having next time."

"The stork brought me, lads!" the admiral insisted. "That's what I was told, and that's what I'm sure happened! On the contrary, Hezekiah, it is the fault of the modern world for telling us men differently. I had no idea until serving five years in the navy that having relations with a woman had anything to do with this! I was an only child, and I thought parents sleeping in twins beds was the norm! If I had been left alone, all of this would have been avoided! I would have died a lonely man, yes, but think of the heartrending letters some illiterate stork would have gotten! Harvey! For the last time, man, pass me those god-blessed chips! How many impassioned speeches does one man have to give?"

Junie relaxed from the contraction and rolled to her back. "I want to push. Tell me it's time! I want to start pushing!"

"Keep your head, woman! We're doing fine, what's your problem?" the admiral said with a strong nod and a chewing on the empty cup the lieutenant passed him. "Nedrick, if this ever ends I want you to write one nasty letter to the head of this supposed medical center for not allowing me to bring in my pom-poms! This is a total disgrace."

Nedrick vehemently scowled at him. "If I write any letter, it will be one forbidding anyone but one man to be with a woman who's in labor! Preferably it will be a man with no stake in the impending birth, and pom-poms will be strictly taboo for a mile's radius! I can't stand any of you any more than I can stand to see Junie going through this!" He turned back to her.

"Isn't this just what Junie needs?" the colonel asked calmly, but disapprovingly. "A communist over there, and a traitor to his friends over here."

"I am *not* a communist!" Downs jumped to his feet.

"You didn't take back the fact that you weren't proud of your country, or did I miss that between your gnashing on that poor face cloth?"

"I am *not* a traitor to my friends!" Nedrick wanted to hit him. He stood erect and turned from Junie to see him.

"Then what's that letter you wanted to write?" Harvey asked as a reminder.

"Harrison, give me that hat!" the admiral yelled.

"Why?"

"Because I need it more than you! Hand it over, man!"

"NO!"

"I'm your superior officer, and I'm closer to the ground! Give me that damned hat, or I'll see to it with my last breath that you're court-martialed!"

"But you're sitting down!" the poor colonel wailed.

"I don't have my pom-poms, and that's all that matters!"

Downs: "Take that back about me being a communist, or I'll give you a concussion right *through* that damned hat, Harri!"

Nedrick: "And don't ever say I turn tail on my friends, you wimpo Harrison!"

Harvey: "Get your hands off him! He's the second oldest fart here, and he's the second highest in rank!"

Crimmins: "Listen here, you sour cream cook, are you calling me the first old fart?"

Harvey: "What if I am? What could you possibly do about it?"

Crimmins: "Besides seeing to it that you're court-martialed, too, I'll just stand myself up here, and bop you in your old honker the same way I was—"

Harrison: "Sit down, you old coot, before you kill yourself on this baby's birthday."

Crimmins: "Hezekiah! Of all people calling me an old coot! Who's the one who has to wear that stupid hat from the communist and won't give it to his superior when told to? That's disobeying direct orders, name-caller, and if Nedrick wants to turn on his friends, maybe he—"

All but Junie: *Shut up, Admiral!*

Downs: "I want it stated for the record that I am *not* a communist!"

All but Junie: *"Shut up, Major!"*

Nedrick: "If we're correcting the record, I want it documented that I am *not* a traitor to my friends! Harrison, if you don't—"

All but Junie: *"Shut up, Captain!"*

Harvey: "Well, at least I haven't done anything they can yell at me for, Junie. Even though I'm going through pickle withdrawal, I think I'm—"

All but Junie: *"Shut up anyway, Lieutenant!"*

Harvey: "Wait a minute! Can't you see that Harri's the one who started all this in the first place?"

All but Junie: *"Hey, that's right!"*

Harrison: "Well! Forgive me for speaking the truth! Can I help it if none of you are man enough to—"

All but Junie: *"Shut up, Colonel!"*

Junie, finally: "ATTENTION!" she called, so upset she actually missed a contraction, and she reached over to use the bulb of the bicycle horn. The arguers jumped, and a few even went into the proper military posture. She was up on an elbow and stared from one to the other.

"*At ease!* And I mean at ease because I want to see each and every one of your faces when I tell you that the minute, *if not immediately,* I am able to walk out of this hospital, I am going to take this baby and marry the first draft-dodger I meet in the street! I will *never* tell you who the father is, and I'll raise this child as a devout peacenik that never pays taxes, never votes, is a litter-bug who burns the flag on the Fourth of July, and wants to do away with every branch of the armed services! Maybe I'll even train him to spy for another country!" She had to relax back, panting, holding her abdomen. She sighed and closed her eyes, feeling nothing but back labor, but enjoying the absolute silence.

The admiral's jaw had slowly dropped. "Men," he whispered, "Take care! She's *possessed!*"

Downs collapsed back in the chair. "Saints preserve us…?"

Junie only panted, tired, already forgetting what she had said. She closed her eyes. They began to realize her situation again, and knew why she felt it necessary to shock them the way she had. They calmed, glancing from one to the other with guilt.

"Oh, I know you're not a communist," Harrison said kindly, patting the major on the shoulder. "And I take it back about you, too, Captain. My apologies to everyone, but especially to Junie."

Admiral Crimmins broke into a smile that decreed them all recovered, and he used his horn lightly. "Quite naturally, it was the tension of the moment, Hezekiah. Entirely forgivable! Greater men than we have succumbed, I'm sure. Junie, what a great few moments of distraction we just staged for your behalf, correct, men? We didn't mean a single word, and I'll give my most fervent prayer that neither did you." He rolled his eyes, her speech being the unthinkable, and he came to take her hand. "Forgive us old coots, my dear. We're the way we are because we care so much about you and the baby."

"It's true, Junie," the colonel added, putting his hand on her thigh and rubbing it.

"We do care," concurred the lieutenant with sincerity.

"All of us, a great deal, Junie," the captain said.

"And we'll do all we can, from here on in," Major Downs agreed, standing with them and patting Harrison on the back.

She smiled, as happy as she could manage. She returned

their support with warmth. "Then, Major Downs, I would like you to do me a favor."

"Yes?" He grasped her hand with both of his. "Name it, Junie."

She nodded, eyes partially closed. "I want you to go out to the van and get the admiral's pom-poms. Do whatever you have to in order to get them in here, but I'd love to see him using them now. On your way back, please get the nurse. Don't take a long time; I'm hoping we're about ready."

His eyes enlarged anew. "Yes, Mr. President!" He was gone before Junie could giggle.

Captain Nedrick took his former place. "How are you?" He stroked her head. She looked as fatigued as he had ever seen anyone, and it worried them all. If his palm hadn't been sweaty itself, it would have become saturated with her perspiration. They all came closer to her with their affection and empathy.

"Tell me I can do this. Please. I don't know any more. I feel like it's not going to end. I almost think I can change my mind! What if this is too much for me? I thought I could do it, but now I'm not so sure. I'm scared. It's gone on for so long; I don't know what I have left. I want to push, I really want to push!" A tear rolled from her eyes, and their hearts broke for her. She moaned and clamped her chin to her chest.

"Junie, breathe with us!" the captain called loudly, they exaggerated their puffing to encourage her. Each wrapped an arm around her and embraced her to give her strength. He took her chin in his hand and brought her from bearing down to look at him. Harvey used the cloth to wipe her face.

"Junie, listen to us. You *are* strong enough. We all know that, and you must believe it now, too, just like you have all your life. You're one of the most extraordinary people any of us has ever known, and you have more than enough love and will-power to do this better than it's ever been done before. You're going to have the most beautiful, healthy, perfect baby that has been born here. We love being your family, Junie. And we love this baby. We're right here, just like you wanted, just like we want to be. You can do this without any more trouble. Come on. Breathe with us until it's time to push." He kissed her forehead the same as she once did to bolster him, and he tasted the salt from her brow. She looked up at them and began to smile.

"There we go!" the admiral shouted, returning the volume to the horn's use. "We're on the right track now. Men to your battle stations! We're going to dock a baby!"

She clasped the arms still holding her face, and she puffed as all the men did with her. When she relaxed, her eyes rolled and closed, but she didn't stop smiling, and she gave them another thumbs-up sign.

"Thank you, everyone. Thank you, Captain. Yes, we're going to do this better than it's been done before! Just let them watch!" She motioned for them to draw near and start breathing with her again.

Dr. Steinmann came in and waited until the contraction passed. After an examination, he said: "I'm going to call the team to set up, Junie and gentlemen. Give us three minutes, and then you've got the green light to push as much as you want. That should coincide with the major's return. I didn't stop to count how many people he bowled over, but they're flattered since he told them he's getting something for the president. Ready, men? This is what all those appointments have been for." He chuckled.

"We're ready, Doc!" Admiral Crimmins called, shaking his fists in practice for his cheering equipment. "Just give us the chance!"

"Elevate the bed for her a bit more while I scrub. We're going to make gravity work for us. You're in good hands, I see, Junie. T-minus two minutes, crew." He left and a pair of nurses entered rolling in the necessary equipment. Colonel Harrison started raising the head of the bed.

"That's fine, sir," one of the nurses said.

At that moment, the door burst open, and they turned to see a panting major fanning himself with what he had retrieved. "Here I am, saints preserve me!" He stumbled into the room with the items and nearly collapsed into the admiral's wheelchair. Admiral Crimmins patted him on the back, kissed the pom-poms, and tooted the horn with glee. The major's breath was heaving, and he turned to use it to help Junie pant.

She held out her arms to him with a smile, and he went to her. "Thank you so much, Major! You should have been in the Secret Service! Come, everyone! I want a hug from each of you before we become parents!" she called. Her hair was matted down, her face pale, and she shook from the strain, but the smile they all needed was there, and they adored her more. Lieutenant Harvey embraced her with strength, and they lifted the admiral to a proud standing so that he could share his emotion. Colonel Harrison had removed the hat and kissed her cheek. She turned to the captain last for the speech he had given her, and she kissed his forehead before releasing him to breathe again. She was nearly sitting up, and she reached for their hands.

Dr. Steinmann returned, and he took the sheet from her legs and sat at the foot of the bed. "Okay, Junie. Start when you feel like it."

She nodded, and they could see from the change in her body and her expression what effort it was taking. She pushed through three long, hard contractions, and when the doctor announced the baby was crowning, she rested back to catch her breath and be taken care of by her friends. They wiped her face, neck and chest, and gripped her hands when she nodded that she was ready again.

"The baby's head is out, Junie. You've got to give me a minute now. Breathe with her, gentlemen. The baby is a very healthy pink, and it's moving its features just fine. With a nice head of hair, I might add."

Junie looked at the ceiling and wanted to smile with the news. They panted together, staying right with her, and then Dr. Steinmann asked for the last action.

"All right, Junie. Finish this up! This baby wants out to meet all its daddies!" He laughed. The staff around him smiled.

She opened her eyes to smile at all of them, and then pulled against their strong arms to a higher sitting. She bore down with more strength than she knew she had. When it was done, she fell back and closed her eyes.

"Here we are! Look at this, everyone! Junie, look what you have here."

It seemed too much to ask her body to move further, and when she didn't hear any sound, she began to feel frightened.

"Junie?" she heard Captain Nedrick whisper into her ear. "Come on, we're all waiting for you. *Look.*" He and the Lieutenant used gentle arms to slowly raise her. She heard a little person working on a very big cry.

Dr. Steinmann was holding up their newborn, umbilical cord still attached, the skin still freshly glistening, and every healthy feature perfect and mobile. "I'll be darned if it's not a boy! What do you know, those steps really work," he said, then laughed with the nursing staff.

The baby's face was round, and he had handsome head of brown hair. He opened his mouth and protested being on display. He waved his fists in the air.

"He's beautiful," breathed the lieutenant.

"What a handsome lad," spoke the admiral in reverence.

"That is one fine looking kid," declared the major.

"The planet has a wonderful new addition," said the colonel.

"Junie, you did a tremendous job," gave the captain. He kissed her cheek. This prompted the others to feel free to do the same.

"Who's going to do the honors?" Dr. Steinmann asked. "Admiral? If we go according to rank, you're up first. How about you this time?" He held up the scissors to cut the cord.

His cheeks were newly tear-streaked, and the pom-poms were dropped to his sides. He wheeled himself over with shaking hands. "I'd be more proud to do this than anything I've ever done, sir. Welcome to the world, son. May your next ninety years be as perfect as your last nine and a-half months and this moment. God bless you." He cut the bind to his mother. They watched as the nurses took the infant and did the work they had to.

"He's breathing normally, his pulse is strong and good, and he's very alert. Ten points out of ten!" one announced. They cleaned him and put on his first diaper and nightgown. She swaddled him tightly in a powder blue blanket. "Who's first?" she asked in turning back to the crowd.

Junie smiled. "This Daddy," she said, pointing to the admiral. "You have another title now, sir." She giggled. She had to laugh as each man had their turn holding their child. When the baby had made the rounds, Lieutenant Harvey handed him to her.

Junie sobbed an elated giggle. "Hello, my sweetheart!

You were worth waiting for, weren't you, our darling? Yes, you were. Welcome to your family! Did you see all those wonderful men? They're going to raise you to be as excellent as they are. You're going to be loved and cared for, and a very happy and blessed man. We love you, honey. We love you so much."

He belonged equally to all of them, and the doctor and nurses cleared what wasn't needed, and left the group in peace. Junie nursed him, and after the baby had been held by all again, they placed him in the little isolate so Junie could be made more comfortable. They kissed her for happiness and congratulations, and because each was stated as the possible father, their visitation rights were as such. They were allowed to stay as long as they wanted, and that early afternoon they all were given a chair so they could nap with the huge smiles that remained on all their faces.

Section Eight: The Aftermath

[19 JUNE, THE FOLLOWING YEAR;
2 AUGUST, THE YEAR AFTER;
25 NOVEMBER, THE NEXT YEAR;
7 JULY TWO YEARS LATER, AND
11 JANUARY, FOUR YEARS PAST]

Junie and the baby went home in two days to overwhelming love and appreciation. Instead of finding it difficult to cope with her recovery and a newborn, she found it humorous dealing with five doting fathers. She was often more a referee than a mother, and remembering whose turn it was to change, burp, walk, hold, and play with the beloved boy needed an appointment book more than the rotations. She couldn't have been more pleased.

Before the first rotation, each of the officers had submitted their choice of names for the birth certificates, and a blood sample for the paternity tests. Before going home, Junie asked Dr. Steinmann to take his time with the latter determination, for it was endearing to her to see each forming a strong bond with the beautiful infant. The baby responded well to each, and from the tenderness he was surrounded with, he was growing to be calm and happy. He was very easy to spoil.

"I love the little tyke with all my heart, but I don't think he's my kid," the admiral said one morning in the kitchen. They baby was in his portable swing as they talked around the work center again.

Junie laughed. "Why not, Admiral?"

He shook his head, squeezing the soft, terry cloth

155

dinosaur with a squeaker inside it. "He's too good! I gave my sainted mother trouble from the word go, as she told me. He's not yours either, Nedrick. From what I can smell, there's no marching to the bathroom going on."

The captain smiled and winked at Junie. "He's not flying planes or steering tanks or whipping up scrambled eggs, either, that I see." He took a sip of his coffee.

"None of that matters. He's all of ours. We may find out who the lucky father is, but I pray we all are fortunate enough to raise him and any that follow him together and the best we can," Colonel Harrison stated.

Major Downs and Lieutenant Harvey had called off the bet made long ago from feeling guilty. They derived such joy from the entire experience, it no longer mattered what the order was. The favorite pastime of card playing changed to babysitting. The admiral wanted children's stories as he held the sleeping infant and Junie read. Painting was done after bedtime. The propagation of a new iris was postponed. The office equipment grew dusty. The lavish meals became geared for Junie's nursing, and they all walked their new love in the pram. Not a peep was left unobserved, and their first month passed so quickly, they forgot the testing was being done or was even necessary.

It was Major Downs who answered the telephone. He returned to the parlor, the camera he had been using yet in hand. "Junie, it's Dr. Steinmann. He says he wants to speak with you. He has the results!"

Lieutenant Harvey was holding the baby, and she stood from her final work on Colonel Harrison's tapestry. All noise stopped, and all eyes went to the peaceful newborn.

She slowly put away her work. "I'd like him, please, lieutenant," she said with a grin. "When I come back, I'll hand him to his father. Be ready, Uncles! Ready, angel?" she asked, kissing the baby's head. "We're going to find out what your name is!"

She was gone only for a few moments, but to the men it seemed much longer. Admiral Crimmins put his hand on the horn and tapped it as a test. Colonel Harrison sat in his chair, gripping the armrests. Major Downs paced in front of the fireplace. Captain Nedrick took his feet off the footrest and put his elbows on his knees after running both hands through his hair. Lieutenant Harvey went to the bar and straightened what didn't need straightening. Though suffering for her return, they jumped when she entered the room.

"Here we are!" Junie's smile was so broad she had to laugh. She held the infant's back against her giggling chest so they could both face the crowd. "I am so happy with the way you've been about this. You're better than I even dared to hope. You're all going to make excellent fathers, and all of these children are very, very fortunate to have you. I have no more doubts at all. Now that we have a name to call our little pride and joy, it will be even better.

"The tests were unanimous, and Dr. Steinmann is going to mail the report today along with a copy of the birth certificate he'll have filed at the hospital this afternoon. Gentlemen, it is with great love that I present to you... Hezekiah Leslie Harrison, Junior." She laughed, and then began to cry tears of gratitude. She kissed the baby and looked to his father.

The colonel was no less than dumbstruck. His eyes took the look of astonishment, and his mouth slightly gaped. He wanted to shake his head, but he couldn't move.

Junie went over and knelt before him. "I'm not making this up, Colonel! You'll see the proof when it arrives. Here is your son, sweetheart!" She placed the baby in his arms and kissed them both. The colonel slowly cradled his offspring, seeing him as if for the first time. Cheers, applause, and toots from the horn swept through the room, and the others congratulated him, and enjoyed the sight of the new couple.

"Hezekiah is a mouthful for a little fellow," the admiral said, coming over to them. A beaming Major Downs took the picture. "Did you have any nicknames when growing up, Hezekiah?"

He nodded, tears of his own coming. He didn't attempt to wipe them away, so Junie tenderly obliged. "My parents called me Zeke until I joined the air force," he whispered.

"Hello, Zeke!" came the call from all gathered.

Zeke Harrison would soon resemble his father. His hair changed to a dark red, and the nose became unmistakable. Four months passed faster than any they'd ever known, with each boasting of check-ups, milestones, fretting over ear infections and injections, and helping with care. The rotations were scheduled again, and soon Junie was back under Dr. Steinmann's supervision. Zeke cut teeth, was allowed to crawl around the parlor and into their laps when they played cards, and he insisted on rides in "Uncle Addie's" wheelchair instead of his stroller. He was taught to use the horn and he did so very well. Cigars became a thing of the past.

Their second Christmas tree had a very elaborate electric railway set around it, but also an extensive fence to keep the expert creeper out. He was toddling at ten months, and his second summer would be spent out in the back lawn, finger painting with his devoted father. The colonel had a pack he wore on his chest to hold Zeke against him, and they presented his mother and uncles many works of art. The house began to fill with these portraits and baby toys, replacing the antiques, oil paintings, and military items. The formerly unused breakfast room became the downstairs playroom, and the driveway was paved in anticipation of tricycles, bicycles, roller skates, and scooters.

"Junie," the colonel said as Zeke's first birthday approached, "There is something I've meant to tell you for nearly two years."

Junie, eight months along with her second child, was taking Zeke in for his nap. "What's that, Colonel? Come on, sleepyhead! You can paint with Daddy later, little darling."

He smiled as his son curled against her and she kissed the round head. "I never once cared if I had a boy or a girl. I didn't say anything because I was against great odds as it was. Just being a father is enough of a prize. I would give my life for him, but you didn't have to make any preparations on my behalf." He put his arm around her and kissed his son, also.

Junie giggled. "Colonel, just between you and me, I don't know if any of those things work. But for you, sir, if you remember, the one time we had our 'BT' after sitting out here in the gazebo, I was totally unprepared and I didn't think stopping to do what I normally did was a good idea! You had a son, sweetheart, because that's what you were meant to have."

Colonel Harrison would remember her words for the rest of his life, and he kissed her before she departed with his reason for living.

Zeke was thirteen months old when his little brother was born three weeks early. Her coaches plus her first son were with her, and the labor seemed easier, though it was as long, as her previous birth. In a month they were gathered in the parlor again when she received the telephone call. She never saw a man cry and laugh so hard at the same time as when she went to the admiral and placed Robert Adam Crimmins,

Junior, in his arms.

Bobby was slighter of build and his hair would be a bright blonde for all of his childhood. His eyes were as blue as his father's, and from his first cry he had the gift of speech. It became a standard household joke to tell Bobby Crimmins to shush, though it never worked. With an older brother to keep up with, Bobby advanced quickly, and they considered themselves fortunate there were so many adults in their family to watch them. Zeke taught Bobby how to climb stairs, and if they were out of sight for more than a minute, they were often found playing with Uncle Major's collections.

Their third Christmas was spent with a smaller tree. The parlor simply couldn't hold the former size and all the presents, the train set, and a higher fence. What Bobby couldn't climb Zeke could, and what Zeke couldn't get under or through, Bobby could. They were perfect together, and just hearing them laugh spared them from a great deal of discipline.

Shortly after the turn of the New Year, Junie was again waiting with her growing family in Dr. Steinmann's office. She now knew before the pregnancy test was read to her. She almost immediately became nauseous, and though her cravings were still not fussy, insomnia would plague her for every gestation. Zeke was twenty-six months old, and Bobby nearing fourteen months old, when she gave birth to her third son. In a month the results would be sent to his father, and then Lieutenant Harvey had a new frame to put up on his sparse walls. It was the birth certificate of Donald Lee Harvey, II.

Donny had sandy blonde hair, light brown eyes, and an oblong face with dimples in his cheeks and chin. His first sound of choice was laughter, yet he suffered from colic, and provided a terrible first few months. The besotted lieutenant stayed up as long as it took, complaining only when the boy grew out of it. Major Downs presented his best friend's son with a Great Dane puppy, and Trumpet became another beloved family member. The three boys screamed with delight in playing with the tawny bundle of energy that would soon be taller and heavier than they were, and Uncle Major even forgave them when they let Trumpet eat two of the goldfish and some of his favorite plants. Trumpet loved to run and wade in the water, and family picnics at the pond were enjoyed at least three times each week if weather allowed. They found a path that the admiral could use with his motorized wheelchair, and the children would take turns riding with him. Their lives had certainly changed.

During the fourth set of rotations, Captain Nedrick announced he had decided to investigate attending law school for corporate practice. It would be a long, meticulous process and he'd start out slowly at first, but he and Junie had become very close, and she had always been supportive of the idea that suited him. Having four others in the house who loved to take care of children afforded her more time to help him study, and hours in the gazebo were spent going over terms, sample documents, cases, and precedents. Her fourth pregnancy was spent helping him with applications and law books. Even on their walks, the subject wasn't often left behind. Zeke and Bobby road their bicycles before their mother and Uncle Cappy, saying they were going to court when their next sibling was born.

Howard Rodgers Nedrick, Junior, was presented to his father less than a month before their fifth Christmas. Ward, as he was to be called, had dark brown hair, light grey eyes, and a square jaw. Zeke was three and a-half, and took charge immediately. Bobby joined in, and Donny, walking as well as the others and never allowing them to forget him, was glad he was no longer the youngest.

The feet that were once so fearfully huge and clumsy on Trumpet were now springs for an accomplished athlete. He was fully grown, with handsome markings and an expressive face. He expertly took over a different son's bed every night, and the affable pet soon made friends throughout the neighborhood. He quickly learned what was right and wrong for the youngest members of his family, and if a child was ever out of sight, they knew an intelligent substitute would be at his side. The men contracted a play yard to be built near the gazebo. Included was a large elevated fort, a swing set, jungle gym, slide, monkey bars, obstacle course, a maze of short tunnels, and a huge sandbox.

It was essential that Trumpet have access to as much as possible, and what he couldn't get into, he could bound over. It was slightly disconcerting to Junie to have his black chin even with the height of her changing table, but both Donny and Ward refused to lie still unless they could pet Trumpet's smiling head while being worked on. When the favored companion came into the kitchen wearing a pouch around his neck, any occupant knew a drink and snack was ordered. With a small reward, it would be delivered with envied cooperation, and a wild wagging of the saber-shaped tail.

Junie had her hands and heart so full she couldn't relate to life before coming to live on Pond Point Avenue. Major Downs was now the only one scheduled, but a fertility test, done at his request after months of disappointments, revealed a count so low Dr. Steinmann couldn't predict a fifth pregnancy. For the first time in years there was depression in the house. Junie wouldn't tolerate it. She encouraged him as much as she could, and shortly after Ward turned one, she knew she would be giving birth to his child.

Alan Taft Downs, II, was the only baby out of the five Junie could greet by name at delivery. The number of them no longer fit in the same delivery room, and Dr. Steinmann took great pains to be sure everyone could be in attendance. With Alan's healthy cry and the confirmation of the paternity tests, their lives were complete. He would have dark brown hair and green eyes, and Lieutenant Harvey gifted his friend's son with a matching dog. Trumpet and Charger made a noble and gleeful pair, and Major Downs admitted he had never been happier in his life. He could still exhibit a wild sense of humor, but he became decidedly more affectionate and calm, and a large bonus for him was that father and son shared the same birthday. He would repeat for years on end that his life could be defined by two days: The date of his enlistment, and July seventh.

It was her last birth for the contract, and Junie was now approaching her third decade. She had witnessed the others grow more youthful, and she suddenly yearned for the admiral calling to her through the intercom, seeing Colonel Harrison with his helmet on, Major Downs teasing them all so well, the captain coming out with her that night so long ago after reading the contract, Lieutenant Harvey teaching her how to do things in the kitchen, and being summoned as Ensign Junie. She said nothing to the men or her children, but as Alan grew, she knew it was time to start scanning for employment opportunities, and thinking about calling her former boarding house.

She held Alan to her, looking at the picture of the gazebo the colonel had given to her long ago. Sighing, she kissed the baby and tried not to let her tears flow.

"Lieutenant Harvey, please pass Bobby and his father the sour cream. We're having a form of vegetables tonight, so, quite naturally, a thorough drowning is called for," Junie said, humorously eyeing her second son and his father. The young boy of almost five years was again sitting in the admiral's lap. "Admiral, I know we've talked about this before, but I still think it would be a good idea if Bobby sat in his own chair when we eat. Most especially at dinner."

"Food tastes better when he's here!" The admiral put on a pout. His son copied him so perfectly, Junie had to laugh.

"Then that will apply to the peas! Bobby, Uncle Louie made a very good dinner tonight, and these peas are fresh. I want to see both of you take a whole spoonful right now. I don't care how much sour cream you have to add, I want them eaten."

"But, Mommy!" Bobby started. He looked up at his father.

"'But, Mommy!'" duplicated the elder Robert Crimmins.

Junie tried not to smile, but couldn't resist. "It should be easy since you're two peas in a pod yourselves! And that goes for the rest of you boys. Little boys *and* big boys! Only Alan has an excuse, don't you, sweetheart?" She rubbed the back of the infant blinking at her very slowly from her side. He tugged on his pacifier, and put his heavy head on her shoulder and closed his eyes. "When it comes time, you'll eat your peas for me, won't you, darling?" She kissed his head with a grin, and sighed contentedly.

So did someone else, which prompted the admiral to smile. "Junie, dear, if I may change the subject just a bit?"

Junie tsked him with a grin, thinking it was a ruse. His ruses were usually successful.

"A discussion of the greatest consequence occurred

today, and I think now is as good a time as any to tell you what it was about. What do you say, men? Let's get to the business at hand."

The captain suddenly stiffened. "Admiral? Perhaps...! I think that maybe... I don't know if this is..." He took a deep breath and shook his head, then collapsed into a flustered silence.

Junie was surprised. It stirred a memory from long ago, and she grinned bittersweetly for that alone.

"Nonsense, boy! We're one, big happy family here! We've always done things this way! Quite naturally, this should be no different. Nedrick, stand yourself up there and take the bull by the horns! Don't beat around the bush! Cut to the chase! Get straight to the matter! On your feet, soldier, and forge ahead at full speed. That's the best way in these situations, and don't we know it!"

Junie looked from the admiral to the captain, who did slowly rise to a standing. He put his napkin in his chair, checked on his nearly two-year-old son beside him in his highchair, and took another breath.

Nedrick cleared his throat loudly. He was suddenly the consummate professional. "Junie, it hasn't escaped our attention that we have only about six weeks left on our current contract. You are aware of this?"

She glanced from one man to the other, a sad grin flickering over her face. She had picked up the telephone many times but had been unable to dial any numbers. "Yes, Captain. It's past time for me to start making arrangements, I know."

He shook his head, not daring to look at anyone. He took a shallow breath. "You've been true to your word, as I hope we all have. The part of the contract left to be fulfilled is your stipulation that after the last child is four months old, you would move from this house. Do you recall that?"

Junie pushed away her fork and wiped her mouth. Her appetite was gone now. "Yes, sir," she replied, and her tone was much more somber. She hadn't addressed any of them this way in years except for a mirthful scolding, but it seemed fitting now. She lowered her face and gave the sleeping baby a long kiss on his soft head.

The captain nodded haltingly, watching her, feeling his own heart ache. "We must give credit where credit is due, Junie. There is something very, very special here. We are one big, happy family instead of just a satisfied contract where we're packing our sons off to military schools with nothing but our names. That's what it might have been, Junie, but not with you. We can't be anything but profoundly grateful. We all care for you very, very deeply. It hasn't been just the admiral for a very long time."

She looked up for a moment and grinned as warmly as she ever had. "I hope you know that I love you all, too. I love you all very much."

"Pretend the table is my horn, everyone!" the admiral called, and the resounding noise of wood being pounded and entire table being rattled was enthusiastic. She giggled as she covered Alan's ears.

After the captain led himself and Ward to participate, he returned to his former demeanor. "It is not our wish—any of us—that you move from this house, Junie. Not even if it's across the street, not even if it's somewhere else on the property. We'd like to keep you here, and…we're willing to take, well, extraordinary measures to ensure it, if you will."

Her face took on a look of wonder, and she would have taken the statement as a ribbing if he hadn't looked so uncomfortable.

Captain Nedrick cleared his throat, straightened his shirt,

and shifted in his shoes. "We discussed this thoroughly—the other officers and I— and what we'd like to do is offer a new contract, so to speak. Not five more children, if you were worried about that," and Junie sighed loudly while the others either smiled or chuckled, "but, a contract of...*Marriage*. After weighing the pros and cons of every officer, we selected one of us to ask, or maybe beg, for your hand." He swallowed, and all around him knew it was a painful action. Junie's eyes enlarged, and she stared at him. He felt it keenly, and his nervousness multiplied.

Major Downs looked at Lieutenant Harvey and they tried not to sound out their laughter. Even Colonel Harrison was smiling this time. Admiral Crimmins tickled his son.

"So," Nedrick blindly continued, "would you mind, Junie Bernice Smith, entering into a contract of matrimony between yourself and... And...myself?"

Junie's posture began to straighten. "You mean...?Captain, you're not asking on behalf of the admiral this time?" she nearly gasped.

He saw only her, and he slowly shook his head. "No, I... I could never do that again. I... You see, there is a serious complication on my part. I love you, Junie. Very much, as it turns out. I tried to be unbiased during our discussion, and I even opted out of giving my opinion more than a dozen times, but I can only thank God they chose me! I would have performed my duty had it not been me, I suppose, but... I probably would have clocked anyone else pretty good first, and I wouldn't have felt bad about it, either. I'm sorry." He appeared worried and determined at the same time.

The four other men looked at each other, some rolling their eyes, and chuckled. The law student had been so true to the contract he had denied to himself what was obvious to them. The mirthful discussion, led by the admiral, had been for his release alone.

Junie closed her eyes as her heart missed a beat. Her face took on a pink shade, and then the corners of her mouth began to hint of a smile. She kissed the baby in her arms once more, and she felt able to soar about the room. She looked up at the captain, who was still waiting for her, and she smiled. As years before, she wouldn't have him feeling awkward. She smiled for him. "Captain Nedrick, since this is to be a contract, I have a few points I'd like to add. Just like before, please."

It was his turn to be startled, and a gaze that was openly vulnerable went to her. "Yes?"

She had at her fingertips what she wanted. It was not her choice to leave any member of the household, but realizing she might be without his company made what she felt in labor completely minor. She had encountered the same serious complication some time ago, she admitted to herself.

"Number One, you must realize I won't be calling you captain anymore. And you won't be calling me Junie, either. It will be names like darling, sweetheart, and honey. Silly things like that. The sillier the better, I think. It goes against military protocol, I guess, but that's the way it has to be. All right?"

Nedrick appeared as if he wanted to cry with relief. "I agree. Darling."

Junie nodded happily. "Number Two, you'll have to become comfortable with affection. I want to hold your hand, or have you put your arm around me, or when we see each other, smile and kiss no matter how many officers are in the room. Do you understand?"

The throat was cleared again. He nodded obediently. "Yes, honey."

"Number Three, no more BT's, FS's, or anything at all

like that ever again. I don't have to explain that, do I, Rodgers?" She held her giggling.

The captain flushed now, and the others chortled. "No, June," he said softly.

"Number Four, you have to love me. Not just now, not just as an item in a contract, but as your partner and soulmate, with no asterisks, expirations, or considerations about other officers."

He nodded. "That is already a certainty, sweetheart."

Junie's eyes shone bright with fulfillment. "You show great promise, my darling! And, Number Five, you may expect that this is the way I'll feel about you, because I will. I… I already do. I do, Rodgers." She stood up, becoming emotional. "I mean no slight to anyone else, but I know I want to follow my heart for the rest of my life and it has H. Rodgers Nedrick written all over it. I hope no one minds." She slowly grinned, looking just to him.

The captain began to smile, finally feeling safe in experiencing what was occurring. "Junie, sweetheart…" he whispered, his joy apparent.

The admiral was the one to celebrate first. "Where is my blasted horn when I most need it? Bobby! Pretend we have horns!" Laughing, a few of the others joined in when they began making honking noises.

Still looking at her future husband, Junie began to laugh, tears dropping from her elated cheeks.

The captain smiled in return. When the din calmed, he suggested: "Honey, Ward will be two in November. How about that date in the parlor, with our family around us, and we'll have a private ceremony? The boys can escort you in, Admiral Crimmins can give the bride away, and if the rest of you would be my best men, I would appreciate it."

Glasses were raised as confirmation. The plan would take

momentum the next morning.

She nodded, loving the ideas he had spent time envisioning. She began to walk around the table to hand Major Downs his sleeping baby. She went to her intended's side, smiling up at him. She took his arm. "Darling, can we walk out and see the fountain, just as we did when you talked about our first contract? We can discuss all of this, plus the fact that I want to give the boys a sister in a few years. You can put that in writing somewhere, too, if you'd like." She giggled. Many around the table joined in.

Nedrick nodded happily once more. "She'll be named for her mother."

Junie reached to touch his face as she had done so long ago to the admiral. "I love your contracts, Captain H. Rodgers Nedrick! But, most of all, I love their author."

He took a lesson from the admiral and grasped her hand and kissed it. "Then it will be my specialty."

Admiral Crimmins broke out with a loud laugh. "Off to the fountain with you both, I say! Let's all hope along, a truly kiss is in the making, which will provide us the perfect opportunity to get out of eating peas, right, my dear boy? In other words, damn the healthy stuff, full speed ahead to dessert!"

"Yay, Daddy!"

"And that goes for every non-pea-eating male in here! We have something to celebrate! Break out the messiest stuff in the galley, Harvey! And keep it coming!"

Laughter filled the house as the new couple went outside. The fountain performed to a most appreciative audience.

In three years, the crowd of them was in the delivery room as Junie gave birth to June Bernice Smith Nedrick. Her husband was at her side, his arms around her, and to her left was the rest of their family. Admiral Crimmins, who would be one of Jannie's godfathers, held up a pink pennant when being shown the infant that said "One down, four to go!" A laughing Junie and Rodgers held up the hands with their wedding bands to show this contract was the only one that mattered now, and then they kissed each other well.

"Yuuuuck!" four year old Ward yelled, looking at his brothers. They all laughed at him. Zeke was a few months shy of his eighth birthday, tall, slender, and keeping his red hair. He was on his father's back, the both of them smiling and waving. Bobby was six and a-half, and sounded so like the admiral that it was often hard to tell them apart. On his father's lap, the admiral's hand was over his smaller one on the horn's active bulb. Donny was five and a-half, and was jumping up and down while holding onto his father's arm, though pairing them by hair color alone would have been simple. Alan, at thirty months, was held on the major's hip. He put his arms around his father's neck and asked again why Trumpet and Charger couldn't be there.

Ward squirmed between the parents he loved, coming to see the tiny bundle that his mother and father were cradling between them, wiping away the perspiration and tears that, quite naturally, marked both.

Epilogue

Hezekiah Leslie Harrison, Junior, graduated with high honors from the Air Force Academy. He married a fellow officer that fall and they had two boys and one girl in subsequent years. Colonel Harrison moved from Pond Point Avenue when his son and daughter-in-law were stationed overseas, finding an apartment near their home. Toward the end of his life he returned to the Federal, where he died in his sleep at the grand age of 104 years old. Hezekiah Leslie Harrison, III, carries on his grandfather's talent for painting.

Robert Adam Crimmins, Junior, joined the navy for a four year tour after high school. He was given an honorable discharge and went into business development. He married, divorced, and married again, having two daughters. The admiral lived to celebrate his youngest grandchild's third birthday, and died after a short illness in Junie's arms on the eve of his one hundredth birthday. The last words from his smiling lips were "Thank you, Ensign Junie."

Donald Lee Harvey, II, became a military chaplain. Upon his discharge from the navy, he and the lieutenant traveled the world as missionaries. Donny married later in life, and his wife gave birth to twin daughters and then a son. While living in Africa with his son and his family, Lieutenant Harvey contracted an illness and came back to be treated in the same hospital where his son was born. It was while there his heart failed him. Junie and Rodgers escorted his body back to his son, and where his father was buried became Donny's permanent home for his church. The family returns to Virginia once a year to see their relatives.

Ward and Jannie Nedrick were raised in the same hamlet as their birth, with Ward studying law and joining his father in corporate practice. Jannie became a surgical nurse, marrying after college and giving her parents two grandsons to spoil. Ward married twice, having with his first wife a boy and girl, then two girls and a boy with his second wife. They bought the house next door to his parents, where they reside to this day. Rodgers retired from his law firm at the age of seventy-five, and spends his free time raising grandchildren and step-grandchildren, and traveling with his life's partner.

Alan Taft Downs, II, was primarily raised by Junie and Rodgers as Major Downs unexpectedly succumbed to a massive heart attack shortly before Alan's twelfth birthday. Alan joined the army, in time surpassing the rank of his father, and named his first son after the man who unabashedly adored him.

For his mother's and step-father's thirtieth wedding anniversary, Alan and his wife invited his five siblings and their spouses to Pond Point Avenue, where seven Great Danes ate twelve goldfish, eighteen grandchildren screamed with delighted play, and one of the most successful contracts ever written was never mentioned.

About the Author

Like most authors, C.C. Troy knew she wanted to be a writer when she was very young. Marriage to Jim Troy and raising three wonderful children postponed the physical application, but the creativity and emotional devotion wouldn't be denied. Today she and Jim live in Arizona on their beautiful "two acres of dirt" where she writes, sews, works on her handyman special house, and, above all, dotes on her four grandchildren.

Other titles by C.C. Troy
Beulah the Bull, Astraea Press (2013)

Uplifting Mil, coming Summer 2014 from TouchPoint Press

Uplifting Mil
Book One

Episode One
"Only you, Mildred Thelma."

Carlotta peered through the worn screen of the back door, knowing exactly where to find her daughter. It was always the same. Halfway down the small, weedy yard toward the river bank, her only child was sitting on an old lawn chair, lost in a book. A stray mongrel lay at her feet, curled in what was probably a rare safe nap.

Carlotta's grin began to twist. Her eyes began to narrow. Confirming her cool maliciousness was her sixty-eight-year-old body: hunched, withered, gnarled, and, in some places, discolored and scaly. She was living proof a brutal temperament could age a person considerably.

For all of her life, the first priority of Carlotta Eloise Ebbert had been Carlotta Eloise Ebbert. She spent her best days promoting herself and demoting others with such flair it seemed magical. Those with remorse or consideration best watch from a distance. No one compared to her. Any challenge to her position was unsuccessful.

Yet, decades later, the only remnant of her dynamic personality was an immature drive to make others miserable. Doing so made her feel superior. Doing so made her feel she still had an impact on the world. Doing so brought back her youth when she had beauty and wit and power, and could easily survive offending a temporary friend or two.

Now she had none. No one called, no one wrote, no one stopped by. She had worn them out. All of them. Except…

The book reader. This was the one person Carlotta would always have in the palm of her hand not because she had earned devotion, but because her foolish child—as Carlotta thought of it---believed in the Ten Commandments. Carlotta took such advantage of her daughter's faith, the angels around them despaired, and the effect her behavior had on her sole offspring had been profoundly damaging.

Carlotta's defense was that her daughter had provided nothing but disappointment from conception. Her lover was supposed to marry her when she told him, but he didn't. Deeply ashamed, he rejected her and ran back to his wife instead. To insult her further, it turned out to be a girl. Carlotta had wanted a boy to name after him so everyone would know, but pressure was applied to name the newborn after her mother. That, too, turned out to be a pitiful mistake. In line with the Catholic upbringing she then shunned, Carlotta's mother forced her to keep the infant, promising help whenever she needed it. However, her mother died just after the baby turned one. That person sitting out there, Carlotta thought every day of her life, ruined everything for me.

She couldn't open the door for the springs groaned too much. If letting it slam closed to rattle her daughter was the only option, it wouldn't work. She had tried that before and failed. She had been the only one upset. No, she'd have to think of something else. It had to be good. The chance to do this didn't come often enough. She surmised it must be a good book her child was reading or she would have been in by now. Carlotta had overslept her usual naptime.

A puff of breeze a little too strong for the early fall day passed by her face, and Carlotta took a quick inhale of breath in becoming nervous. She nearly stepped back in case her offspring was disturbed. The grown child might glance toward the door in wondering if her mother were up and required assistance. Her daughter either didn't feel it or didn't take note of it, for she merely turned a page.

Stupid, stupid, stupid! Carlotta thought. Her life is going by just like that. No, not going by. Gone by. Done. Finished. Wasted. At thirty-two years old, her daughter might as well be older than her. She looked it and acted it. She had to be the most boring, meek, homely person on the planet. Carlotta was ashamed of her. She might as well have given birth to... She couldn't think of anything bland and despised enough. This child was totally devoid of personality, humor, or interesting features. Carlotta scowled, her hand tightening the grip on her cane. She had decided before her daughter started school they couldn't be related. Her real child was out in the world, wealthy, a model, teasing a different lover every night. It wasn't this thing.

Carlotta grimaced, and then glanced at her arthritic hands. Slowly the solution to her immediate problem came to her. Their landlord had promised weeks ago to replace the old door and he hadn't yet, of course. But she had her cane and that might work. She knew her idiot offspring would fall for it. Carlotta smiled.

She took her cane with both hands, put her feet as far apart as she could, and then raised the cane. She set her balance carefully for the blow could tip her over if she wasn't cautious. Though her face was contorted with determination, she had full view of the reaction she anticipated with such delight.

"MILDRED THELMA!" she yelled at the top of her lungs as she smacked the cane against the metal door jamb. The collision rang hollow, loud, and piercing. She even dented it, and the reverberations hurt her joints. Carlotta was already pleased.

The small dog yipped and sprinted for the trees. A man by the dumpster was startled. Mil jumped so her book fell from her hands and she nearly toppled from her chair. She took a breath to calm herself and stood, anxiously embracing herself as if she were chilled. Her head was held low and she kept her winced gaze down. To any onlooker, she appeared to fear a blow to her person.

She cleared her throat. "Mother, I'm sorry. You're up."

Carlotta rolled her eyes and made a tisking noise. "Congratulations, moron! It's not enough for you to be the ugliest person in the world; you have to be the stupidest, too. Why don't you take an hour to try to figure it out what you should do next? I don't mind. I have nothing better to do. I love watching you fail at everything."

The caustic resonance of her mother's voice was always worse than what she actually said. Mil felt the prickle of embarrassment burn her face, and she turned away to retrieve her used paperback. She folded the lawn chair and brought it toward the apartment complex. She didn't look in her mother's eyes. Mil never looked into anyone's eyes, most especially her own.

Carlotta stood in the doorway, both hands now clasping her cane for dear life. If she moved she would fall. In hitting the door as hard as she did, she couldn't regain her balance. She didn't have the strength to correct it. She stayed frozen in place, silently terrified, hoping her daughter would arrive in time so she wouldn't collapse.

Hospitalized twice already for falls, she had hated every moment there. Nobody appreciated her presence. She was a delicate, exceptional beauty who moved with grace and spoke with charm. For no obvious reason, they treated her with disdain. They were supposed to be professional and tolerant. Here she had been merciless in her criticism for their own good, and they acted otherwise. They, including her daughter, deserved the disrespect they got from her. Now in fear of returning where she considered herself mistreated, Carlotta's breathing turned shallow. She began to shake; her frail muscles straining to their capacity.

Mil put her book down and gently took her mother's shoulders to lead her to a walking position. "Be careful, Mother. Some of the floor tiles don't stick anymore." Once her sole parent had safely taken a few steps, she went back to recover her reading material.

Terror gone, Carlotta's scowl returned. "You read too much," was her thank you. "Only stupid people read! I never read a book in my life. I was too busy doing things. I was out traveling, meeting people, shaking up the world! You've never been out of Derby! You have no idea what the next town looks like. Who lives their life like that? Only you, Mildred Thelma. Only losers like you."

"Yes, Mother," came the automatic reply. Mil led her to the small kitchen table in the small kitchen, in the small one-bedroom apartment they shared in Derby, the smallest city in Connecticut. They had rented here for over thirty years. When the senior Mildred Thelma Ebbert passed away, Carlotta brought her toddler here when the building was complete. Being the original tenants of their apartment, they had out-lived or out-lasted four owners and a remarkable seventeen landlords. This was the only home Mil knew, and, being as introverted as she was, it was one of the three houses she had ever been in.

The two Ebberts were on the ground floor of a colonial-style house that had eight apartments for rent. To move in above them it seemed the requirements were insomnia, anger, and obesity, judging by the noise and footsteps that could be heard all times of the day and too often the night.

For the first ten years they had signed a lease to allow the privilege of living as such. After that, it was forgotten, and on the first of each month, the landlord came knocking on their door. Mil paid him in cash and was given a handwritten receipt. This was an understanding that was passed from one landlord to the other. As far as Mil knew, they were the only tenants that were treated this way.

The kitchen had the same tired cabinets, the same dreary paint, and the same outdated appliances. The small refrigerator was the newest, having been replaced twenty years ago. This one also had to be defrosted every other week, and it rattled when a fan came on somewhere in the back. The electric stove was clean for Mil was a tidy person, but the bulb inside the oven had burned out, and it was so old a replacement couldn't be found. Two of the electric burner knobs had been missing for ten years, so she didn't use those when she cooked.

One of the past landlords had replaced the fixtures on the sink, but they didn't fit the openings, and if she wasn't careful, water would flow against the wall and into the lower cabinet. She was sure there was mold down there. Combat with cockroaches and ants never ceased. Only three of the windows operated, and the carpet and padding had been scuffed down so far they could now say they had hardwood floors.

However, there were two outstanding features which gave Mil tolerance for everything else. The first was they had their own private entries. Theirs was the only apartment that had a front and a back door all to themselves, and this was so important to Mil it didn't matter that their main entry was nearly all the way to the left of the lot, ten feet from the dumpster. She never had to meet anyone this way, and whenever she took out the garbage, all she had to do was peek out the little front window to be sure she was alone.

The second feature was the back of the house where she just was. She could step out that screen door and be in a yard that skirted the Naugatuck River. The Naugatuck wasn't a major waterway, for it wasn't wide or deep even at its greatest point. It was more a creek than a river in most areas. Locals would rather point out the Housatonic River, which the Naugatuck flowed into farther downstream. The beautiful Housatonic hosted docks, expensive houses, and water sports because it made it out to the Atlantic Ocean. However, to Mil, the little Naugatuck was more than fine and what kept her here. Looking out the back door, the kitchen and bathroom windows of the only home she knew, she saw Eden.

It was her Eden alone, for the lawn consisting of weeds was infrequently mowed. She had attempted to put in a garden, but it was vandalized within a week, and she hadn't tried it again. There once was a BBQ stand for everyone to use, but that too had been damaged, and the stand that supported it bent over. The dumpster was always being set on fire, cars were stolen a few times a year, and the stockade fence had graffiti on it.

Once while she was out reading and the kids came to add to the harsh words, she dared her shyness and to ask them please not do such a thing. They laughed and sprayed all of the first floor windows. The neighbors were enraged: It wasn't her fence, but the windows were a part of their places, and now they looked awful. It was her fault and the current landlord demanded she fix it. Mil did. She worked on every pane until they were as clean as the day they were installed, but it took her a very long time. Her mother had sat outside while she scrubbed, and made ridiculing comments for the duration.

Yet, there are those who are born with an indomitable flicker of hope, and Mil was one of them. Contrasting her low opinion of herself, she had faith there was abundant joy and beauty in the world. She had the ability to be happy for others, and though she herself could never take part, she was unshakable in her belief that God paid attention.

So it was that Mil could sit outside for a weekend hour and enjoy ducks paddling by, birds coming for a drink, and abandoned pets resting in the grass—some of them answering her calls to be friendly. Last fall she was pleased a Great Blue Heron visited for two days. Sometimes the sun sparkled on the water, hurting her eyes in a wonderful way, or the sunset would make it look colorful and moody. There were times she knew it had a current, and other times it seemed to be waiting for her to decide what it should do. Some tried to fish, and though no one ever swam there, she did see vagrant men splash water on themselves often enough. During a truly hot summer day, she would go wading if she dared go that far from her needy mother, and it always made her smile.

"Brush my hair," Carlotta said and brought her out of her thoughtful mood. She elbowed her as severely as she could.

Mil winced with the blow. "Yes, Mother."

"What are we having for dinner tonight? It had better be good."

She hadn't considered a menu yet. "Sunday dinner should be special."

"Why?" Carlotta sneered. "What's so special about Sunday? Why do people feel they have to have a special Sunday dinner? Because they went to church? I thought church was supposed to be its own reward. But, let's celebrate it, Mildred Thelma. All those nice, godly people who don't know you or care about you, who don't invite you to their houses, who don't ask you to join their little groups, oh, yes, make a special dinner in their honor. We'll have a toast to your stupid ideas.

"Heaven wants beautiful people, Mildred Thelma. Not you. When you die you're going to be just as alone as you are now. And you should be! There's no Heaven for people like you. There's no ugly cherubs. They don't help you now, they won't help you later. God doesn't care one iota about you or He wouldn't have made you this way."

Mil kept her gaze aimed at the floor. "You shouldn't talk that way, Mother," she spoke quietly.

Carlotta guffawed at her. "I'll talk any way I want. I've never been afraid of anything or anyone, and I don't need anything or anyone, including you. Especially you. You're pathetic. I know exactly what you do at that stupid church of yours. You sit in the back. All the way in the back, in the darkest corner, and you don't say a word to a single person. I'm right, aren't I? You don't have to answer, you loser."

St. Michael's Roman Catholic Parish was not only an easy walking distance, but the size Mil was comfortable with. The early Mass was the least attended, with the 11:30 a.m. service delivered entirely in Polish due to the large immigrant population that settled there. However, just this morning Mil had to move to allow a late male congregant plenty of room, and she had decided to change her usual spot.

Carlotta had waited for an answer, but there was only silence. She burst out laughing. She knew.

They slowly advanced to the single bedroom, the distance not being far. In the center of the ceiling was the light fixture. It was a globe with four light bulbs. When Mil snapped on the switch, she was reminded that one was burned out. In the room were a vanity table and bench, a dresser, and two built-in closets. Against the far wall was one of the windows that wouldn't open. It was oddly elongated and toward the ceiling. Beneath it was a twin bed. One and one-half of the closets were Carlotta's; filled to the point of damaging the clothes it held from being so overstuffed. Mil hung everything she owned in the second closet.

The dresser was Carlotta's and so was the bed. Mil had slept in two types of beds her entire life: A crib and an Army cot. There wasn't room for another bed, but it was fine as now Mil didn't believe she could sleep on one. It stood propped up in a corner, only set up at night, and it abutted Carlotta's mattress.

Carlotta moved herself to sit on the vanity bench, and she clicked on the yellowed make-up lights arching around the wall mirror. She gazed at herself and smiled. She saw a woman twenty-one years old, with flawless skin, fetching blue eyes, dimples when she was happy, and silky auburn hair that begged men to touch it. Her eyelashes were naturally thick and flirtatious. She spent her money on clothes and jewelry for herself. She knew exactly what to do and what to say at all times. Men always looked at her twice. They remembered her. She was the one that got away. She was the one they pictured when they were with someone else.

Mil took the greasy, orange-dyed hair out of the top bun and let it down. It was thin and stringy and should be cut, but her mother wouldn't hear of it. The ends were frayed and pieces continually came out when worked. She kneeled behind the bench and reached for the antique horse-hair brush. One hundred strokes was the rule when her mother was growing up. The same rule was in force today. It took

Mil twenty minutes every single day to brush Carlotta's hair. Now it was the last thing that should be done to it, but her mother had an uncanny way of being able to count even when she was talking. From the top of her scalp to just beyond the seat of the bench, Mil began to stroke.

It soothed Carlotta. By stroke twenty or so she closed her eyes and had a peaceful aura come over her face. Her posture slumped the more. Mil couldn't brush the hair against her mother's back for her knobby spine stuck out too much, and it would eventually be painful. Carlotta had advancing osteoporosis, giving her the classic curved-back appearance. It was the main reason she was high risk for a fall. Her balance was always pitched forward.

Mil had to take the gloopy hair in her hands and brush it this way, on top and underneath, which was unappealing. One hundred strokes. Exactly one hundred. Sometimes it felt like a million and her arms, back, and knees ached. Sometimes she thought about other things and her mother would snap that she had gone past the number and couldn't count. By the end her fingers would be numb, but she always managed to finish.

"How many men missed out by not knowing me?" Carlotta said to a collection of black and white photos framing both sides of the age-spotted mirror. Most were pictures of her favorite Big Band singers; some were actors of her era who had played romantic leads. "All that you had, but you missed out on me. I could have set the world on fire for you, my babies! You would have been even bigger than you were. Maybe you'd be jealous because it would have been me that got most of the attention once the press got to know me, but we would have been the envy of the world. They would have said your greatest talent was finding and keeping me." Carlotta laughed. She looked at her daughter by route of the mirror.

"Yes, Mother." Stroke forty-one.

"I took care of myself. I wore silk hose when others were stuck in knee socks. I smoked cigarettes with a holder when others had to share. I was always two pounds underweight just to be sure, and my waste was the tiniest of everyone I knew. Even my mother knew I had IT. 'Carlotta, you be careful, girl. You ooze attraction, and it's the devilish kind!' she'd say to me. 'You only have to walk by and you drive them all senseless!'" Carlotta nodded. "The Father in our church had very interesting confessions to listen to because of me." She delighted in herself.

"Yes, Mother." Fifty. Half done. She shifted on her calloused knees.

"And then," and here her smile always fell, "there's you." Her eyes became lit with hatred.

Mil focused on the hair in front of her.

"How could I have a child like you? I am beautiful. Your father was the most handsome man I ever saw. Look at yourself, Mildred. Stop that and put your face over here."

As Mil knew, this always occurred at sixty strokes. Always. She paused the brush and decided to enjoy letting the blood flow to her hands as she lowered her arms. She leaned forward to put her reflection next to her mother's as had been demanded of her countless times. She didn't look at the mirror.

Carlotta shook her head. "It should be against every law of nature to have a child as ugly as you when the parents are good looking! There must have been a mix-up at the hospital. Why I didn't check that out is the real sin. Look at you, Mildred Thelma. You have grey hair. All of it grey! At your age! You don't have a style. Part it in the middle, push it behind your jug ears.

"Your teeth are crooked, so is your nose, and your shoulders are too round. Do you have a waist? Your entire body is without any shape! I could knock down more whiskey than ten men put together and still hold my own, but you? Chocolate milk would put you under the table. You wear flat shoes, old clothes, and you've never driven a car. Never. You're tragic. No wonder you never got asked out. Did I tell you I tried to bribe one of your classmates to take you out? He laughed at me. He said there wasn't enough money in the world!"

"Yes, Mother." Mil paid more attention to the ends of her mother's hair. It seemed to taper into nothing, and was uneven. Since she wasn't allowed to trim it, she'd have to let it fall out. Stroke seventy-two.

"Good thing I never was interested in grandchildren. You took care of that. After having you, I didn't want to see another child born into this world. It's their fault!" she said, waving her hand at the photos on the mirror. "One of you should have found me! You should have known I was out here, ripe for your picking! But no. You lost out. You all lost out. They're sorry now. And you, too, Mildred Thelma. Had I met any of them, you never would've been born.

"I'd have had smart, attractive children that did things with their lives. I wouldn't be living in a dump where the only pet you have is tramp. I would have shaken the dust off my shoes from this crappy town, that's for sure! I could have had it all. I should have had it all. What I got was you. I never did anything to deserve this, anyone would tell you. I am a person who requires the best."

"Yes, Mother." Stroke eighty-five.

"In a way I'm glad you're dowdy. You'd beg to wear my clothes. Never would I let you! Over my dead body! You're too stupid to wear jewelry so I don't have to worry about that, but I've hidden my collection. You'll never find it. Go ahead, turn this place upside down, clean it all out, you won't find anything. Think of it, Mildred Thelma, I have thousands of dollars' worth of diamonds, emeralds and rubies, and you'll never see them. You never will! I made sure of that."

"Yes, Mother." Ninety-six. Ninety-seven. Ninety-eight.

"Don't even ask me where I put them. I will never tell you. Just think about that when you go to bed tonight."

"Yes, Mother." Mil sighed, feeling worn. She stretched to put the brush back on the table top. "Would you like to go to the bathroom?"

Carlotta frowned sternly at her. She gathered the brush and tried to hit her with it, but she was in an odd position and she couldn't move well enough. As she wouldn't drop one of her most prized possessions, she held it out for Mil to return it to its rightful location. Mil did. "Did you give me the stool softener last night or not, hoping to cause me trouble?"

Mil slowly went to her feet. She rubbed her knees. "I gave it to you, Mother. You get it four times a week, and last night was one of your nights."

"Good. Don't think I don't know what you're up to. I have my eye on you. Get me in there. Goodbye for now, my babies! I'll see you boys tomorrow. Hurry up, you clumsy ox! You know once I ask I haven't got much time!"

Mil helped her to a standing and gave her the cane. Carlotta passed gas the entire walk, cursing at her and the builder for making such narrow passages and doors. She would call the new landlord tomorrow and complain about a number of things and imply that it was her daughter that made her call. In the little bathroom, Mil put the raised seat on the commode, and she helped Carlotta gather her one-piece dress.

Carlotta slapped her hands away. "Get out of here! Get out! Leave me alone, you imbecile! Be ready when I call. I'll need a good clean up. I already started, and it's your fault!"

Mil nodded. "Yes, Mother."

Carlotta snorted. "'Yes-mother- yes-mother!' You don't even make a good copycat!"

Mil shut the door and went back to the bedroom. She sat on the bench of the vanity table and pulled the small wastebasket to her feet. It was her routine to clean the hairbrush while waiting. The hair left her fingers greasy, and if she didn't rinse the brush soon the bristles would discolor further. She'd have to do that later as there wouldn't be enough time now. In returning the brush to its proper resting place, a string of red rosary beads caught her eye. They were hung on the side of the mirror's frame. When she looked toward the necklace to think her respects, she caught sight of herself.

She lowered her eyes immediately in shame. She was plain, she knew it. Frumpy and mousy, she was this and all of the other bad words that could be used to describe her. She had no fashion sense, and didn't know what to do with hair besides keep it clean and out of her face. The bun she put her mother's hair in each morning stayed only because of the overuse of bobby pins. She and her mother could have been the same size, really. The expensive outfits would have been odd on her. She knew nothing about accessorizing, the rules about colors and seasons, or even what some articles of clothing were for. Every day it was the same style of drab, loose dress, except for weekends when she wore dull slacks. Those were polyester. She was overweight, but she had no athletic abilities so that hardly mattered. Round face, no taste, tight budget. This was her own description. Mil believed no effort spent on herself would make a difference, so there was no point in trying.

The two-shelved linen closet was in the hallway and she went to find what she would need to cleanse and change her mother when she yelled for her. She'd better not go anywhere else, she knew. Her mother would purposely make a horrible mess if she didn't come instantly when summoned.

Mil decided they would have tuna casserole and biscuits for dinner. It was her mother's favorite.

******

Mil paused to recheck her mother's surroundings before going out the door. Carlotta was sitting on the sofa watching their small black and white television. Beside her Mil had placed the walker, the portable commode, a pitcher of water and a plastic cup, a plate of crackers covered by a used piece of saran, and a box of tissue. Her noon pills were in the pill organizer marked with the day of the week. With medications dispensed, lotions applied, and sundry items at the ready, Carlotta was set for the day. Even the local channel of the television was prepared for immobility as it was manufactured before the invention of remote controls.

They never exchanged hellos or farewells. For years not a single sound or gesture was made when Mil returned or departed, so she just exited. She had one key in her purse, and it was without a key chain. She locked the door behind her and stepped cautiously over the broken flagstone walk and headed for the street.

Derby Avenue, or Route 115, was a good location for those needing public transportation. On weekday mornings the bus came by every twenty-two minutes, and Mil never missed the 6:22 a.m. pick-up a few blocks from her apartment. She didn't start work until 8:00 a.m., but she didn't like a crowded bus, and she must sit by a window. So afraid was she of having to sit next to another human being, she would rather leave appallingly early than take the chance of sitting beside anyone who might notice her.

As in church, she had an exact spot she made a bee-line to. She always took the seat where the tire well blocked half of the foot room. This location guaranteed no one could sit beside her, and since the tire well took three rows to rise and fall, more often than not, the seats in front and in back of her weren't selected either. Mil was so dependent on this row should her chosen spot ever be taken, she would have been paralyzed about what to do.

But, thankfully, that never happened. The ridership was sparse at that hour, and what made it sparser was that the nearest coffee shop wasn't open for another nine minutes. Most waited until the latest trip possible, even if it meant they'd have to stand, and even though they could have made their coffee at home. To Mil's common sense, this was very silly indeed, though in this it came to her aide.

Today was a good day as she took her favorite seat, put her purse and grocery bag beside her, and leaned over the tire well to peer out the window. The route never altered, even in bad weather: north on Derby Avenue, a left on Division Street, and at the third stop after going down Division, she got off. Mil's stop was on Maple Avenue, right in front of the emergency entrance to Griffin Hospital. As small as Derby was famed to be, it had its own hospital, and Mil had been employed there all her adult life.

Mil disembarked and walked down Maple to Spring Street, passing another bus stop filled with awaiting passengers, and went by the shipping and receiving area of the hospital. Over several blocks here Griffin had many buildings of associated medical offices, but the one she was headed for was a red brick building on the corner of Spring Street and Seymour Avenue. Totally unmarked and industrial looking, the former storage building held only two things, and those were the medical records and bookkeeping offices of the entire complex.

As cruel fate would have it, Mildred Thelma Ebbert was one of the most scorned of all medical personnel: a senior accountant in the billing department. After taking a single unit of study in high school and doing exceptionally well, her mathematics instructor mentioned her knack to his aunt who worked in the aforementioned brick building. Mil was offered a job after graduation and trained on site. This was a blessing for Mil as she never would have been able to subject herself to any kind of interview.

Now in the fifteen years she had worked there, it could be counted on that Mil knew every contracted insurance, their complete contact information, and each company's allowables, modifiers, and procedure codes. Take-backs and write-offs were child's play, her work had never been audited by an insurance company, and she always knew what to charge for a single ear swab and the nursing assistant holding it. As she never took a day off, was more than punctual, and could put in any hours needed, there wasn't an employee more valuable than she.

Even so, it was more than likely she was the most overlooked staff member in the history of her workplace. Her utter inability to socialize made advancement impossible. No one beside her individual office knew she existed. When being sent the customary acknowledgement for fifteen years of service, the hospital president asked if there was a mistake because he had never heard of her before then. There were no words to describe her. For Mil, however, this was perfect.

She walked by a single row of parking spots for no more than ten cars, and up the short stoop she trod. The locks automatically opened at 7:25 a.m. On average she had a half hour to wait. She didn't own a watch, but a buzzer sounded when the locks disengaged, so she knew when it was time to go in. There hadn't been an operating business day in the last dozen years that Mil wasn't the first one inside.

What Mil did while she waited was a mystery even to her. She never thought about it anymore. It was as if her brain shut off and she became lifelessly suspended until she heard the buzzer. There wasn't anywhere to sit, so she stood next to the door and directed her eyes to the street. She didn't notice anything. She didn't go over a list in her head about what she had to do either at work or at home. She didn't solve problems or worry. At first she prayed, but prayer for her was an intimate practice where she closed her eyes and felt in the company of her Savior. Doing so in a public area would make her vulnerable to anyone walking near, and she didn't want to be nervous in front of Jesus. He wanted her to love all people, and instead she was afraid of them. She had apologized, and stopped years ago.

Though she never remembered the half hour, she didn't try to, either. One time when the buzzer sounded and the locks seemed to slam over, she was shocked to find herself facing the door going over its wood pattern. This couldn't happen again as someone could have been standing behind her without her knowledge. Words could not describe the terror she felt in the realization. She made it a point to be more careful, but once her brain deemed her body was properly positioned, it appeared to abandon her until the buzzer made her jump. It never failed. No matter the weather, there she'd be, seemingly a statue, so quiet and so motionless, living merely for the purpose of getting through that door.

With the lights automatically turning on in every hallway, she made it to her office as the building awoke for the day. Office number #123 was her home away from home. She opened the door and turned on the overhead florescent lights. They blinked and clicked as they sputtered on.

There were five desks in her office, with one area walled off from the others. This was where her manager sat all day. They had a coffee pot, a small refrigerator, a microwave, and down the hall were vending machines. If they wanted, they could walk a block or two to the hospital cafeteria, but Mil had never been there. Her employee badge was buried somewhere on the bottom of her purse, unused since the day it was given to her. She packed a lunch every day. Others did go because the employee discount was very good, but once she was in the office, she didn't leave until it was time to go home. That was at 4:30 p.m. She even limited her trips way from her desk: Precisely at 10:30 a.m. and 2:45 p.m. she went to the nearest bathroom. There were only two stalls and she found this time to be consistently not busy. She always used the second stall.

It was Monday and Mil took a new plastic container of instant coffee out of the grocery bag she had toted. She supposed her coworkers thought the hospital provided it, for no one ever asked to share in its purchase. She didn't drink coffee herself, so this confirmed to the others that the new product had to be a bonus from their workplace. They did know, however, that no other office got the same treatment, so they thought they were special and didn't dare risk it by telling anyone else.

Mil started the brew and then went to her desk. She had the largest desk in the office. There had been times this embarrassed her, but for the workload she handled it was decided long ago she had earned it. The person who declared that had been the office manager; the aunt of her mathematics teacher who helped her acquire the position. That aunt now was retired, and with her went all of the cordial treatment Mil had ever known. Now she worked under someone else.

The desk was wide and long and appeared impossibly heavy. It was solid wood with three desk drawers on either side. On the worn surface there were in-boxes, out-boxes, a small calendar with the same picture of the hospital for every month, her computer monitor, an adding machine, a solar calculator, and a plain, black plastic holder for pens and pencils probably as old as the building. There wasn't one personal item. The chair was adjusted to her height, but other than that, it appeared spotlessly clean and orderly, awaiting an occupant.

The right corner of her desk was left open. Mil tried not to see it, and the empty space wasn't of her choosing. This was where the supervisor always sat when he came to speak with her or host an office meeting. She had attempted placing an assortment of items in the way, but he always brushed them aside without care. Not a day went by without him taking his perch, whether he had anything to say or not.

George Valkass was the office manager. He sat in the walled off area most of the day, talking on his cell phone, laughing, playing games on the computer, and often shaving and grooming himself. He was overly handsome, six years her junior, single, and was paid far too much. Mil did his work along with her own, and instead of being grateful or apologetic; he enjoyed punishing her for it. He was conceited and juvenile, took all the credit, and considered it a bonus to be able to ridicule others, especially her. Not wanting to be a target themselves, it appeared everyone was either entertained by his hostility or unbothered by it. So stoic was she that it never occurred to them she was a human being; that it was wrong, or it could be troubling her.

It was true Mil was accustomed to being harassed, but it was not true it had lost its sting. Her mother and her boss, the very people to admire and trust the most in life were, in her case, the worst people she could be in the company of. Perhaps it was dumb luck she was born to Carlotta Ebbert, but it was Mil's submissive personality that garnered her Mr. Valkass. She had the seniority to transfer, or the grounds to have him removed, but she lacked the self-esteem to raise her voice. And so, day after day, Mil went from Carlotta to Mr. Valkass and barely survived by reading a book in the weedy backyard she thought of as paradise.

There wasn't a window in office #123, but long ago someone had tacked up a large travel poster of Bermuda. This was to Mil's left. Every day she made sure it was securely fastened, and then she stood before it to admire the colors of the blue sky and water, the green palms, and the pink sand. Pink sand, she always marveled, studying it. Pink sand! Stretching for hundreds of yards was a pastel beach with bright white buildings. It was beautiful and peaceful and it calmed her, but after this glance she didn't dare notice it again. She feared the poster may be taken down if they knew she liked it so much. Burying herself in her work, she didn't think of anything else until it was time to go to the bathroom.

When her fellow billers came in, it always seemed to be in the order of how they sat in the office. For such a small microcosm of people, it was strange that nearly half of them took the bus. Thompson Gates did, and he was the first one in most of the time. Mil already had her adding machine humming when he entered, poured his coffee, then sat down at the desk nearest her. He never greeted her, but he did talk to himself. If he forgot his lunch, had a fight with his wife, or wondered if his beloved New York baseball team was going to win, Mil would know in short order. Six months away from retirement, Thompson was counting the days. "Another day, another fifty cents," was what he'd usually mutter.

Colin May came in next, also the courtesy of public transportation, and he was whistling as he often did. Mil didn't know the tune. He was the youngest member of the #123 team, and the most unflappable of the group. Nothing bothered him and he assumed nothing bothered anyone else. He always thought there was a solution and always said so during any meeting when errors were pointed out or problems arose. The trouble was all his solutions were completely wrong. This became secretly valuable to Mil for she knew doing the opposite of what Colin said was the right answer.

"Hey, Thompsie. How was your weekend?" He went to the coffee pot and took too many packets of sugar. Thompson hardly ever answered him, but this made Colin laugh and he sat down and sipped his coffee too loudly as he did so. He would always say a cheer for Thompson's rival baseball team, chortling at his coworker who held true to form and showed a scowl as his answer.

Tony Thorne was next to come in, and he put his jacket over his chair. "Mornin', guys," he called, meaning everyone, but only got a reply from Colin. His next two words were always about the weather. "Warm today!" or "Rain today!" or "Windy, huh?" or "Snow's comin'!" And then, without ever missing a single morning, he would report that "I need new tires for the old wagon soon," and he'd shake his head sadly. He never bought them, and never asked if anyone knew of sales. He and Colin might talk for a short duration about something in general as their desks were beside each other, then they'd roll their eyes at their work load.

The second-to-last to arrive each day was Lisa Grey Pattinson. Mil liked Lisa and if she were to dare list anyone as a friend, it would be her. Lisa was polite to her and she would say "Now, now, now!" to Mr. Valkass if he began to tease Mil while she was there. However, Lisa was the senior auditor for the entire building, and though her desk was in #123, she was often in other sections doing what had to be done. She and Mil were the same age, though no one would ever think so. Lisa had a set of identical twin daughters and a young son, eight and five years old, respectively. Mil liked the family pictures Lisa had on her desk, and it was the children Mil asked about if they ever had the chance to speak. From there, Lisa could talk for long stretches without needing Mil too much. That was Mil's favorite type of conversation.

Today Lisa sat down, punched in, and called a soft "Hi, Mil!" Mil nodded without smiling or looking at her. Lisa put her purse in a desk drawer, and then collected the few items she always took with her to another location. "Have a good day, everyone," she added, and then was gone. Mil missed her, always wishing she had the courage to greet her more genially.

At precisely fifteen minutes past eight: "Good morning, best Griffin crew," came Mr. Valkass's exuberant call as he strode in. "Good work is going to happen today, right? Right! Remember, your most important job is to make your boss look good!" He laughed. He and Colin slapped palms as he walked by. "Am I punched?" he'd ask under his breath, and Colin would confirm "Right at eight as usual!" without hesitation. Mr. Valkass would always swerve around with a flair and give him a thumbs-up sign.

The greetings he received were wide in range. Tony enjoyed him as a boss and acted as so, Colin thought the world of him and committed time card fraud several times a day for him, and Thompson gave him a mediocre wave of his hand without looking at him. Lisa, when she was there, always said hello after she caught her breath from viewing him, and Mil never acknowledged him at all. Mr. Valkass always paused outside of his door to look at her. She was engrossed in her work and only had eyes for her adding machine.

"And there's the love of my life! Mildred Thelma Ebbert! The name is like music, isn't it, fellas? When are you going to meet me again, Mildred? Don't torture me anymore! Should I tell everyone what wild escapades we had a few weekends ago? Don't let her demure looks deceive you, boys. When she's not confined to these cinder block walls she is a demon, I tell you! Lucky you, Thompson. You get the sit the closest to her."

Laughter sounded as Mil hit buttons on the adding machine. She checked her tabulations.

"I got you a gift, pumpkin pie." He threw his leather jacket and car keys into his office. From his briefcase he took out a long, narrow item, triangular in shape. He went to his spot on her desk and sat. "Everyone come here and see what I got especially for Mil, the one I get wet dreams for at night, and sometimes during the day. Why else do you think I need that office in there? The walls keep me from attacking her as I want to, and as she wants me to, I should add, but, thankfully, with the walls being mostly glass, I can still ogle at her."

All but Thompson had to get up from their desks to come for the view. Mr. Valkass put the item down in front of her. Mil's fingers froze. It was a name plate. When everyone read it, they chuckled.

"Sugar dumpling, let me read it to you." He lowered his voice and spoke in an intimate tone. "'Mildred Thelma Ebbert, Expert Biller and So Much, Much More'. What do you think, lemon cream pie? I know firsthand it's true!"

Mil stared at the desktop, burning painfully with embarrassment. She could barely breathe. Her face felt extremely hot and her eyes swollen.

"She's speechless," Mr. Valkass said, and the crowd laughed. "Tell them, sugar cookie. Tell them that you dream of me, too."

Mil couldn't move.

"She didn't deny it! She's the type that says no and means yes!" There was more laughter. Mil felt there were many more in the room than three others. "It's always the quiet ones, isn't it, Colin? They're always the best!"

"Yes, sir!"

"I expect to see this on your desk from now on, carrot cake. You'll break my heart if you don't, and we can't have that, can we? Mil? Answer me. Can we?" He leaned toward her. He picked up a pen and threw it at her hair. It bounced off her and fell on the floor.

Mil slowly retrieved it. "No, Mr. Valkass," she whispered.

"That's my girl! Back to work, everyone. The rest of you men stay away from her today. She's all mine! Every grey, wrinkled, baggy inch of her!" He puckered his lips and made kissing sounds, and they all laughed. He got off the desk and went into his office. He returned with a large stack of papers that he put in her in-box, "Before the end of the day, sponge cake," then chuckled as he shut his door. He made himself comfortable and began texting on his cell phone. Mil didn't look, but she knew he was watching her. She didn't touch her gift.

The others returned to their desks and began their duties for the day, forgetting about her. With shaking hands, Mil began punching numbers again and wished it was 10:30 a.m.

Made in the USA
Lexington, KY
14 August 2014